THE IVY STAYS GREEN

SOUTHERN SHORT STORIES

by

Janet Brice Parker

INKWATER PRESS

PORTLAND • OREGON

To
My husband, Eddie,
my sons, Brice and Joe.
And to the memory of my daddy,
Clarence Brice.

Table of Contents

ATTIC SPACE

The Cheneys were not your ordinary family. At least not to my youthful way of thinking. They lived in a huge house, deep in the woods outside of our small southern town. The house was named Greystone. That in itself was extraordinary. The only houses I knew about that had names were in books or the movies.

There was something very different about that house and its occupants. They seemed sort of "old world." Maybe like people who lived in England. I had never been to England, but I felt that I could go ten minutes out of town and be transported into a different time and place.

Billie Cheney, who was my mother's best friend, was beautiful and petite. She looked like Dinah Shore and her husband, Buddy looked like Gregory Peck. It all seemed so exciting and romantic.

The house had a library. The idea of a library in someone's residence, was another deviation from the norm. The two libraries I frequented were, the limited one at our school, and a small room lined with books at the combination fire department and civic center.

The library at Greystone was a cavern-like room with deep red, brown and green colors. It had a massive desk, a few chairs and an antique sofa. Shelves hugged the walls and books extended to the ceiling.

The thick books repeated the colors of the room and made a very serious statement.

The library was also a home office for the strict father in that intriguing family. I surmised that the secluded area was an arena for family meetings and discipline sessions.

This rock house with an enormous porch had been in the family for generations, and it's original character was preserved in an exact fashion.

In winter, fires crackled in every room. There was no central heat or air condition and no television. Buddy Cheney wanted it that way.

Fires were stoked and maintained by Shine, the Negro man who worked for the family. I remember seeing Shine haul wood and poke fires, day and night. I'm not sure what Shine did in the summer, but my vivid memory is of that man with his black skin leaning over the fireplaces. Orange flames lit up Shine's moist head and arms. He seemed quiet and kind. I don't remember his saying much of anything.

Geeva, on the other hand, did a lot of talking. Geeva was the housekeeper and babysitter. She maneuvered her large body as slowly as she spoke in her deep, Black southern dialect. Anne Cheney was exactly my age and the best friend I had in the world. But Anne's best friend was Geeva. Anne sat on a stool in the kitchen and received sex education from this woman with eyes as dark as the night.

Anne related to her friends, the things that Geeva taught. Things none of us had ever heard of before.

Our family's lives had been intertwined long before the Cheney children and I were thought of. Daddy and Buddy were friends at a young age, and Daddy dated most of Buddy's sisters at one time or another. After Daddy married Mama, our two families spent time together. That association offered the opportunity for Mama and Billie to establish a close relationship which is strong to this day.

Memories of Anne were locking themselves in my mind when we were three years old. I remember our being placed in a baby bed together when the adults were having a party. Anne stuck a feather in my nose. She wanted to share that soft, fluffy prize with me.

I accepted her generosity and reciprocated with another feather, pulled out of a pillow. From that moment on, we began a sisterhood that was strong, even through adult years when our visits were few and far between.

In my youth, I anticipated time spent in the Cheney house with Anne and her three sisters. Eventually, four other children would be born into the family. The sisters were close in age and all of them talked like Geeva. Slow and deliberate.

The girls read books that were beyond their years. They knew about the classics and poetry. Each girl could play the piano. Culture ran through their veins, because their parents made sure of it.

Upstairs, a long hall, flanked by bedrooms and bathrooms led to a screened-in sleeping porch. The porch was a perfect place for children to camp-out in the summers and listen to night sounds. Many secrets were shared and ghost stories told while we piled up on creaky beds and giggled ourselves to sleep.

Greystone was heaven to me. I was unaffected by the lack of modern conveniences. Maybe that's because I didn't live there. But throughout my childhood and teenage years, I longed to be part of an environment so different from my own.

Christmas at Greystone seemed like perfection seen only in a painting or read about in a book. The house was rich and warm in it's colors and antique furnishings. The beds were tall and soft. Warmth from the fireplaces filled the rooms and the smell of wood smoke was intoxicating. Billie's handmade quilts were a feast for the eyes and beckoned me to wrap myself in their luscious, thick patterns.

Every December, a giant tree was cut from the Cheney property and placed in the spacious living room. The thrill of feasting my eyes upon their tree started my Christmas off right. No one had trees to compare with those of the Cheney household. They rivaled department store decorations in Birmingham, the big city nearby.

All of the ornaments came from Europe, and there were literally hundreds of them dancing amid the colorful lights. They cascaded from the star on top to the huge pile of gifts beneath. The delicate ornaments were made of wood. Wooden teddy bears and angels. Little wooden pieces of art that represented everything pertaining to Christmas.

A large dining room with an impressive table was the family's evening gathering place. When meals were served, every child was required to be present. Adults and children discussed intellectual topics. Opera, the ballet, literature, past and future trips to London and New York. Everyone in town knew not to call the Cheney household at suppertime.

Greystone had an attic. Not the pull-down stair kind. It was a secluded area at the very top of the house, with a real floor that spread out long and wide. A heavy door, varnished to a high gloss, shone in the light of the hall window. It opened to stairs that led to the most wonderful, exciting place I could imagine.

The girls were accustomed to spending time there whenever they wanted, but I did not have access to such a magical place where I lived. When we ascended the tall wooden stairway, I relished every moment of being in the midst of air that was thick with intense fear and pleasure. I felt as though the spirit of some ancestor might appear at any moment and chills ran over me in the heat.

The attic had a window which overlooked the family's beautiful English garden. The long musty room was home to trunks of all sizes and they spilled over with treasures from generations back. Old clothing for playing dress-up, musical instruments, rusted by time. Ancient toys and dolls. It was all so intriguing, I could hardly contain myself. Anne sat on a little seat and looked out of the dusty window. She seemed deep in thought and her mind's eye probably passed through the garden into her imaginary world.

As an only child, I never considered that being part of a large family could have it's drawbacks. It never occurred to me that children needed time to themselves. Anne didn't always go to the attic to play. She went to think, read and be alone. I lived in a modern house. I didn't like it as much as the Cheney house. But I had my "attic space" anytime I wanted it. I didn't realize my advantage. No one bothered me. No one took my toys or my clothes. And no one interrupted my reading.

I often think about the Cheney's literal attic when I need time alone. Time to recreate, write or paint.

Long periods for thinking, or not thinking. Time that stretches endlessly.

"Attic space" exists in our imaginations. It is and will always be, paramount to the creative soul.

WRONG NUMBER?

The ringing of a telephone. A common occurrence in most homes and businesses. The sound can evoke feelings of anticipation, concern or downright annoyance.

Most of the telephones in our house are old fashioned rotary dials. Big heavy receivers that make a long conversation physically uncomfortable. But we like the design of them. We slide our fingers around the dials and retrieve memories from our pasts. We do own a touch tone phone for times when we reluctantly need to check our bank or credit card balances. Computer voices send you through a circle of more computer voices. On the rare occasion when the electronic circle opens a tiny crack and allows an actual human being in, chances are that the person will direct you through a maze or perhaps another circle. It's the system I suppose. Frustrating and futile.

My husband, Eddie and I do not have call waiting, caller I.D or any of the extras. My alternatives to these so called amenities are as follows: Call waiting: They will call back. Caller I.D.: Listen to the voice on the answer machine.

I work as an artist in a quiet studio at home. I am surrounded by woods and nature sounds, so a screaming telephone can at times alarm and disrupt creativity.

A number of years ago, I automatically lifted the receiver to quiet the ringing in my head. I was either disappointed or glad that the call was a wrong number. Six years is a long time and I don't remember my mood on that particular day. I don't remember my mood yesterday.

"Essie?" "No," I replied. "Is this Essie Turney?" the voice was curious. I guessed the woman to be in her seventies with a slight speech impediment. "Well...I'm sorry, Hon." "That's OK," I assured her. She called again in a few days. Same question, same litany. she called and she called. My patience was wearing thin. "NO, this is NOT Essie." You have dialed the wrong number again!

The next time she called, she was breathless. She obviously did not care if I was Essie or not. "I got ta take ker uh deese young-uns an Billie Ruth's next door gettin' ready ta have uh baby an I keent drive an nem kids is runnin me crazy an I keent see cause I ain't got no glasses an she's gonna have thet baby an I don't know who to call." By this time, I was convinced that this whole thing was a prank. My response..."You have the wrong number."

The wrong number lady called again in a month or so. She didn't mention Billie Ruth or how all that turned out. she did, though, mention her sorry son-in-law who was in jail. She talked about her daughter, Jeweleen, who worked all the time, dumped them babies on her, and how "tard" she was. "Tard" from the babies and "tard" from hauling wood for her only source of heat. She shared ailments known only to females and I began to question her age in my mind. It didn't matter a whit to her that I was not Essie or, whoever. She told me bits and pieces of her life. "You have the wrong number." "I'm sorry, Hon."

The calls continued, and after about a year, I asked her name. "Winnie. Winnie Smith." Winnie told me about Donnie, her first and favorite grandson. "He don't belong to thet sorry ol' son-in-law. His deedy left em. I told Donnie when he's growd up, he ken whup boaf em deedy's butts."

Winnie told me she had been married for a long time. Her husband, Harley, wasn't well. He had suffered a stroke and "couldn't walk too good." She talked about the work they had done together. When they were stronger, the two of them worked for the city. They planted trees, bushes and flowers around buildings and in the mediums that ran ran down the middle of two-lane roads. Winnie took pride in the contributions that she and Harley had made. Because of the two of them, tall trees and colorful flowers bloomed around the city.

Winnie could read "a little" to Donnie but she couldn't see too well. "I know I keent say du words rite ya know it...dey jus don't come out rite sometimes." For months she told me the same stories over and over. I got bored, felt trapped and wished I had never started talking to her in the first place.

In the middle of the night, Winnie Smith called asking for Essie. I was short with her in my startled, yet groggy state. She said that she was at the hospital with Harley and he'd had another stroke. She was distraught.

Several weeks later, I found out that Winnie was a widow. "I so sorry, I said."

Some days I was equipped to listen to Winnie. Some days I was not. I judged her mental capabilities and decided that she probably didn't notice or care. I was to find out much later that she sensed when she was intruding on me. This was a person with a face I had conjured up and a mentality I had evaluated.

Approximately three months went by without a call from Winnie. "What could have happened to her? What if she had died? I thought about her every day and was truly concerned about someone I had never met and someone who was, for a long time, a source of irritation. "Oh my word! she is never going to call. I am worried sick!"

On a pleasant summer night when Eddie and I were having supper on our screened in porch, the phone rang as it usually does when we sit down to eat. "Hey, Hon." "Winnie! How are you? Where have you been?" "Aw, I been oar et mu baby brover's house, den I wuz oar et Jeweleen's. I wanted to call you but I taught it uz long distance. My baby brover's wife got Alltimers an she done went off fer tree weeks an didn't nobody know whar she wuz. You give me hope, Hon, ya know it?"

I sent Winnie a birthday card because she called many times to tell me the month and date of this passage in her life. I slipped five dollars (not too much, not too little) into the card and she did receive it. I had distrusted her ability to give me her correct address. I distrusted her neighbors who I had judged along with Winnie. After four years, she has that very five dollar bill in a place only she and I know about. "It'll go to Donnie," she whispered.

My wrong number friend may have hinted for a birthday card but she never asked me for anything. She never asked where I lived or what my husband did for a living. She mentioned once, in her passing comments which usually ran into other comments and opinions, that she wished she could buy a television for Donnie, but she "reckoned she couldn't afford it."

We had a TV we didn't use. I wanted to maintain the mysterious nature of this whole bazaar comraderie we had established. I didn't want to see her and probably most of all, I was afraid for her to see me. I wasn't ready to relinquish my identity and take a chance on her becoming dependent on me. I had a lot to learn. I devised a scheme. My friend, Kate and I would drive to her house. I would sit in the van with a hat pulled down over my head while Kate carried the TV in. I didn't see Winnie but Kate expressed sorrow over her living conditions.

As time went on, and our "wrong number" conversations continued, I asked questions which prompted Winnie to talk about aspects of her life other than her narrow focus I had listened to repeatedly. Winnie really loved Elvis. Elvis and Jesus. She owned a framed picture of Elvis and it was her "prize." She was as in love with him as she had been when she was a teenager.

Winnie talked about picking cotton and other crops, mowing yards to pay for her husband's funeral and about being born in the back of a truck on a day when her parents had set out to work in the fields. She went to school when she could. Winnie seemed strong. She talked about Elvis a lot, but mostly she talked about how God was protecting her and her grandchildren. She talked about her European heritage, the property her house was on and how she wanted to leave what little she had to her grandchildren. She told me about being out of underwear one day and putting on her husband's "Fruit of the Looms." She said that they pulled and twisted and felt awful. We laughed together hysterically, through the phone lines. She told me about the boot leggers down the street, her sorry son-in-law, her husband's last days and his last words...and her sorry son-in-law.

One rainy day I listened to Winnie express grief. For the first time, she cried on the phone. Just quiet sobs. She tried to hide them by interjecting humor between low whimpers. She missed the ones she had lost— her husband, her daddy. I discovered that she is two years older than my fifty three years, not the seventy-something I had imagined.

Eventually, I became less afraid of "getting involved." I wanted to meet Winnie and I wanted her to see who I was. On an icy winter day, Eddie and I loaded the back of his truck with wood and drove to Winnie's. We drove up beside her small, rundown shack. The square wooden building had large cracks between the boards. Winnie, or Harley, had awkwardly patched some of the holes with scrap pieces of salvaged plywood.

Winnie wore sweatpants, a man's coat and a scarf tied around her head. In a stooped position, she was gathering small sticks. She was unaware of our impending visit. I got out of the truck and said, "Hi, Winnie, I'm Janet." Winnie, with a big smile across her round rosy face said, "Long time no see."

The three of us unloaded the wood. Through her grateful, toothless grin, she apologized for liking to dip snuff.

Winnie is warm now. I know because she has called every day to tell me.

I dial Winnie's number sometimes. It's no longer a one way street. I find myself longing for her humor and simple wisdom. "Keep yoar hopes higher than yoar downs. Stay busy an don't thank about thangs. Ain't tat rite, Hon?"

"Do not forget to entertain strangers, for by so doing some people have entertained angels without knowing it." Hebrews 13:2

LOOK AND SEE

Dick and Jane were white. The first grade book with the soft red cover, introduced us to a whole new world. Reading. We stumbled over words, became friends with them and began our journey toward freedom. But we were already free in ways I knew nothing about, until I met Rita.

I plopped my plaid book satchel on the screened-in front porch and thought about an after school snack. The living room of our bungalow house was small. High windows rested over bookshelves, which cradled the fireplace. At three o'clock in the afternoon, the sun, veiled by flickering dust particles, created a misty pool of light on the floor.

Bathed in the filtered light was a little golden brown girl in a soft blue sweater. She was on her knees, with her elbows propped on the top of an ottoman. I was mesmerized. I walked over, bent down and looked into her big beautiful dark eyes. I hesitantly took her silky small hand in mine. She did not pull away, but smiled at me.

I patted and stroked her tiny fingers. Her hair was polished and braided. It shone brighter than my black inner tube in ocean water. Rita's mother, Nannie was our new housekeeper and Nannie would be bringing her young daughter each week. It was going to be a good summer.

My Western Flyer red wagon was perfect for pulling Rita and her choice of toys. We went around the block and became an anomaly to neighbors. As far as I was concerned, she was mine. My best friend and my little sister. We played in the sand box and I pushed her in the swing.

Occasionally, Nannie brought along some other children. Relatives, I suppose. The yellow Jonquils were blooming outside our kitchen window. A mama dog had crawled under the house and produced ten puppies. All of us were reveling in the spirit of spring and curiosity. I reached for the hand of a boy about my age. Then, a heart-stopping voice in my mind came from generations back and continued into the present like an echo. NO! I felt disappointed, confused, helpless and sad.

I thought a lot about Nannie, her husband, and Rita. Sometimes they traveled, but where did they stay? Where did they eat? I gazed around the restaurants we frequented. I looked at water fountains and restrooms in department stores. I could read. I had learned from the Dick and Jane book.

I was young with no knowledge of history, but something seemed terribly wrong. My little "sister" could not go to the swimming pool with me or get ice cream at the Dairy Queen. She would have to enter a side door that led to the balcony at the picture show. I wouldn't be able to put her in my lap, hug her close and watch cartoons.

Years went by and I never stopped looking forward to that one day a week with Rita. My parents moved us into a bigger house up on the mountain. Rita and I took walks in the woods, had picnics and slid down the grass on flattened out cardboard boxes. We lived in that special secret world that children share. We sat on the roof of our mountain house and looked out over our town. From that lofty distance, we saw no lines of delineation. No neighborhoods labeled according to race. Everything ran together and looked the same from our vantage point.

When the day was over, Mama drove Nannie and Rita home. I always went along for the ride. I took mental pictures of wooden houses with tall steps leading to high porches. I wanted to go inside Rita's house, but never did. I waved at dark skinned children and wished I could stay to play with them.

Rita talked about going to church. Sometimes she sang songs I didn't recognize. She clapped, danced and gyrated in a way that made me feel happy. She talked about how her mama smoothed her hair with an implement which had to be heated on the stove. She bathed in a galvanized tub. Rita liked for me to lie on the bed and hang my head off so she could brush my hair. Her simple movements and gentle hands felt good on my head. Rita talked about becoming my "maid" when she grew up. The words made me sick. I did not want to be served by my friend.

I had gone through the customary removal of my tonsils. It was as normal as the chicken pox. I didn't worry about Rita's upcoming surgery. Tonsillectomies were part of being a kid in the 1950s.

The phone rang in the morning. It interrupted my imaginative concentration and startled me in our quiet, only-child home. Mama picked up the receiver and said, "hello." Her long silence frightened me. I sensed something terrible. I heard her low, choking sobs and they told me everything. She hung up the telephone and stared through me. I knew. I lost all feeling in my mouth, arms, legs. Mama's eyes were red and all she said to me was, "We need to get dressed."

I went to my room and saw my face reflected in the mirror. White upon white. Sweat running out of my pours and a scream that would not come.

My best little friend was dead. My tonsils had been taken out and I was still alive. It couldn't be real. I was too young to handle feelings like that. I wanted to get in my red wagon and fly down the driveway. I wanted to plummet down the mountain, tangle myself up in vines and Kudzu. I burned to be thrown and tossed by rocks and branches.

I was desperate to feel the pain, to hurt and scream to the top of my lungs. To find the other side of suffering, where freedom would blow in my face and cool the fire of anger in my soul. Dick and Jane would reach out their dark hands to mine and change the world forever.

In Memory of,
Rita Diane Stockdale

PORTRAITS

Mike Patton was the cutest boy in first grade. That observation was agreed upon by most of the girls in Miss Lula Belle Wilson's class. I was not the cutest girl. Jadie Lynn Tolbert rightfully owned the title. I used to think that if Mike and Jadie Lynn grew up and got married, their children could be movie stars.

In 1950, we weren't concerned with A.D.D. or A.D.L.D. If anyone was "challenged," it was to a game of Checkers or Old Maid. I believe, though, that I might have had something I'll call "Attention Diversion Disorder." My attention was diverted from learning arithmetic to observing faces, colors, clothes and anything beyond the classroom's wall of windows.

Girls who lived out in the country, wore homemade flowered skirts with their brother's plaid shirts. These combinations looked wonderful to me. I wanted to go home with those girls, sit on quilts beside their fireplaces and smell delicious woodsmoke. I wanted to ride horses and help them tend to the farm animals.

Jadie Lynn Tolbert wore her church dresses to school because her mama let her. I wasn't allowed to mix patterns or wear Sunday dresses during the week. But, I wanted to do both. Somehow, dress-up clothes looked appropriate on Jadie Lynn. Her golden hair glowed and her attire glowed right along with her tresses. Jadie Lynn had a face that called for the best.

I memorized Mike Patton's perfectly sculpted features and wondered about the differences in people.

Individual school pictures were taken every year. I dreaded delivery day, when the photographer's packets arrived. In my six year old mind, the white packets were giant stacks of score cards. Those envelopes contained raw truth of the physical labels that were placed on us by our peers. It was fairly easy to trade pictures with the girls and even a few of the boys. Images of the good looking popular kids were snapped up like hotcakes.

Being shy was a pain. I carried the burden of timidity as if the whole world was watching my every move and critiquing me to the very core. The fear of asking Mike for a picture was equalled only to having the local doctor, give me ether.

I pondered my loss. I did not own a picture of Mike Patton, and probably never would. My desperation prompted me toward Daddy's desk. I opened a drawer and pulled out a fresh piece of typing paper. With a newly sharpened pencil, I crawled under the desk, a favorite childhood cubby hole, and carefully began to draw.

Crouched there in the quiet on the cool wooden floor, I did not know this was to be my first of many representations. I listened to the compelling sounds of pencil upon paper, unaware that the lines I made were mapping out my future, my life's career.

Satisfied with my work, I took the drawing to Mama. "Who is this?" I asked. "Why, it's Mike!" she answered.

I will never know if Mama knew my drawing or my heart, but on that day in 1950, my mother's answer gave me joy and confidence.

Forty eight years later, I cannot do math or spell without the help of a computer. But I often wear flowers and plaids or Sunday dresses when I feel like it. I paint portraits and with every brush stroke, appreciate the differences in people.

SELLING DIRT

The very first time I saw twins was in Elmore's ten cent store. My eyes were focused on the glass popcorn machine with red decorations on it. A golden light poured over the already golden popcorn. I could taste salt and feel the squeaky crunch between my teeth. Imagine the warm red and white box in my hands.

I must have been staring at this process too long because I was startled as I looked up. Mama had warned me about crossing my eyes for too long and making faces that could cause me to stick that way forever. I was having double vision and it was my own fault! Two identical faces with blonde curly hair said, "hi" to me, in unison.

Oh, what had I done?! I ran out of Elmore's, across the street and into the safety of my daddy's office. He explained the phenomenon to me and I became fascinated. I began to pretend that I had a twin sister. I spent time in the back of a closet, talking to my image in a mirror that was propped against the wall.

The twins, I soon discovered, had after school jobs at Elmore's and their names were, Linda and Cinda. I couldn't think of a single name that rhymed with Janet, so I figured I was better off going it alone and staying out of the closet.

Spending time in Daddy's office downtown was a treat. I liked the small narrow building with a counter that separated work from visitors. I felt very important being privy to a variety of office supplies. My favorite was the typing paper with Daddy's name at the top. I pressed rubber stamps into juicy black ink pads and watched images appear like magic on the white paper.

As I walked from the front of the office to the back, partitions separated the facility into clean, messy and downright filthy. But I didn't mind. I breathed the smells and remembered them. Standing there among the clutter in the back room was something beautiful, dark and mysterious. It was a safe.

The shiny black vault had belonged to my great grandfather and was ornately embossed in gold with his very own initials, JAB. Almost the same as mine. I was fascinated with the big box and had the idea that it would be great in my room. My collections could be safely held behind it's heavy door. Comic books, Kleenex box inserts with Little Lulu's picture on them, bottle caps, cereal and Cracker Jacks prizes, balls of aluminum foil, empty spools.

The bathroom in Daddy's office was so small, a person could hardly turn around in it. It had a string pull light and a dirty sink. Along the window sill was a dusty collection of cleaning supplies and a wrapped roll of toilet paper. Daddy had rigged a toilet paper holder out of a coat hanger. Mama told me not to sit on the seat.

Beyond this necessary room was a back door that led to the outside. The door was only a few feet from the railroad tracks. The doorknob on the door was gritty with dirt, purple carbon paper residue and blue ink. Years later, when Daddy retired and before he sold the office, Mama and I discovered, under layers of grime, a beautiful crystal doorknob. It now shines and sits proudly in a glass cabinet in our living room.

I was allowed to "work" for Daddy and earn a dime. I pressed stamps into a pink wet sponge which was placed in a dish. When I had put stamps on enough envelopes, I got my dime and ran across the street. My feet stepped on the small squares of white tile that spelled out, "Elmore's" in little black tiles. I reached for the brass bar and opened a heavy glass door that led to our small town's fantasy land.

I shuffled my feet along the unshined wooden floors. Getting lost in everything that was available was the best part. Finally giving up my dime for one little thing seemed sad. I almost always bought a Little Lulu comic book because I knew I could read it over and over and make the experience last longer.

Daddy's secretary was usually a girl just out of high school who stayed around long enough to get a husband. I watched as they chewed gum and typed at the same time. They flitted out the door, their blurred full skirts leaving after them. One of them said, "See ya later alligator" every time she left the office. I could tell she got on Daddy's nerves.

After Linda and Cinda, the twins, graduated from high school, Daddy hired one of them to work for him. He said that she did a good job and was very smart. I often wondered if Linda and Cinda were playing tricks on Daddy, and taking turns coming in to work. If one of them had a cold, or just wanted a day off, then the other one could come in. Daddy would have never known the difference.

At the beginning of the school year, every student was required to fill out a form. The questions were always the same and included, "Father's Occupation:" I was never quite sure exactly what he did. The painted sign on his office window read, "Brice's Real Estate," but I wasn't sure what that meant.

Daddy loved to tease, but I didn't appreciate his humor until I grew up. Some of the answers he gave me concerning his occupation were, "I'm a Broker. "What does that mean?" I asked. "It means I'm broker than anyone else." "Aw, Daddy! Come on. Tell me, really. What do you do?"

"I tell ya what you put on that piece of paper, Daughter. You tell them, I sell dirt."

I took his answer so seriously, and was envious of the children whose daddys were farmers or mailmen.

When I was in my early teens, Daddy decided to have his office at home and rent the one downtown. We had moved into a larger house and he was territorial about one of the rooms, which he deemed, his "den." This private domain of his became very important when my mother's sister came for visits. Sometimes we wouldn't see him for days.

The "den" became the home office and a home office was not my mother's idea of home. Before I knew it, Daddy was back downtown with all of the good old office smells and clutter. Mama was free to talk on the phone with her friends and walk around in her nightgown without wondering if a business man was coming to the door.

Daddy is eighty-seven now. He has a home office. I guess he is allowed one at this stage in his life. Mama goes about her business at the other end of the house.

I admire my father's interests. He sits at his computer and learns everything he possibly can. He talks the talk with my husband and sons. If he is not reading a book, he's listening to one on tape during his daily walk. He is youthful, witty and busy.

Daddy doesn't seem to miss the ink pads and the 1950's Underwood typewriter. I am the one who is nostalgic. I have the typewriter and other memorabilia in my own home office. Even now, he is involved in the real estate business.

I don't have to fill out school forms anymore. But if I did, it wouldn't bother me in the least, to write on the dotted line, that "Daddy sells dirt."

FAMILY TIDE

Papa Brice awoke at 4:00 a.m. A daily routine that he never once considered altering. He read a few verses out of the Psalms, while ice cold water filled the claw foot tub. He stretched, took several deep breaths and stepped into liquid that would have given the average person coronary stoppage.

James Alexander Brice reclined in the tub, letting his bald head plunge beneath the surface. He scrubbed, rinsed and emerged feeling invigorated. He dressed in a stiff white shirt, tie and new gray suit. He tied his freshly polished shoes and briskly tapped down the back stairs to the kitchen.

Papa took a pitcher of orange juice from the ice box, poured a glass full to the top and drank it down while standing over the sink. He walked toward the front door, gave his fedora a tap and took a cane off of the hall tree. My great-grandfather did not need a cane to help him walk. Such an accessory made a man look distinguished, important. At 4:45, this disciplined man left his large family home and started on his walk. The same path every morning, the same distance.

Verbon Brice must have been awake. Papa saw a light shining from the back of his nephew's house. So many Brices and Bains and Stevens. So much history. He saw his sister, Flora's small brick home in the distance. He passed by his brother, Joe's rambling wood house, which was close to the railroad tracks. Joe was not an early riser like James. They were different in a lot of ways.

The only departure from a daily ritual that began years before, was that he walked toward town. He checked the time on his gold pocket watch, and kept up his pace. In the breaking light of day, he could see the painted sign at the top of the brick building which read, "Brice's Department Store."

Papa Brice looked around at the empty two story building. The smell of cotton seed, fertilizer, feed sacks and food items lingered in the stuffy air. Oily dark floors had been worn down in spots and formed yellow hues throughout the structure. Reminders of patrons, farmers and friends who rattled and squeaked into town on their horse drawn carriages.

The cool vacancy, echoed years of owning the general store to support his wife and nine children. He was not an especially sentimental man. This was merely an end before another beginning. James Brice, pulled the large door shut and finalized the past with a click of the old rusty key. A key to pass on to the next proprietor.

Miami. Papa had taken his young family on many trips to the south of Florida. Days of traveling with his wife and numerous children in their bouncy Buick. They'd stop in Cross Creek to visit Papa's brother, Boss Brice. But Cross Creek had cool winters. So, the family piled in the Buick and headed on down farther south.

My great-grandmother had been dead a long time. The children were grown with their own lives and plans. Miami Beach sounded good and warm and exciting.

Papa Brice shared a 1930s cottage with his second wife, Ada. The ample house shaded by lush palms, was within walking distance of the beach.

Every morning Papa Brice walked to the sea and met the foamy waves head on. He swam in the salty water and lingered on the sand. His deep brown smooth color went from his bare feet to the top of his bald head. He was not young but he was handsome and fit. In the afternoons when he donned starched white shirts and light weight slacks, he was the epitome of what life without winter could be.

I was only four years old, but I remember my first visit to my great-grandfather's house. I did not like the dress Mama insisted that I wear. I wanted to join the neighbor children who ran freely in bathing suits and shorts. I knew that the closest thing I had to shorts was my underwear. I thought if I could just get out of that dress and wear my underpants, it would be almost like having on shorts.

I pulled my dress up and nearly had it off when my mother and Ada screamed in horror. Ada told Mama that I was getting buck naked and carried on something awful. My cousins and I never liked our step great-grandmother, and I think the feeling was mutual. We called her "Ada Potato" behind her back, and took delight in thinking our clever expression was the ultimate slander.

My parents were planning a lengthy vacation and Daddy preferred not to stay with relatives. "A vacation was just not a vacation if you had to stay with kinfolks." I would just have to wear the dress and wait. Wait for the motel on the beach with jalousie windows and an ocean breeze to lull me to sleep. Sand for building castles and a huge inner tube for riding the waves. Days stretched before me that seemed as endless as the expanse of beach and ocean beyond.

The T-shirts stacked in my suitcase were restricting in my opinion. I was required to wear one over my bathing suit every minute the sun shone on my strawberry-blonde haired fair little body. A hat covered my head when I wasn't in the water. Mama believed these T-shirts would protect me from "getting blistered." but I still remember feeling stinging arms, and legs against cool sheets at night. I desperately wanted to have black hair and olive skin so I could spend all day in the sun.

Every summer the three of us traveled to a beach somewhere. Daddy often chose Daytona where we unpacked our things and settled in for several weeks. It never took long for me to find temporary playmates. These friends came and went, but my sinking feeling when they left was always the same. Exchanging letters and postcards lasted for a while but eventually evaporated along with my loneliness. There would be more summers and new friends. The cycle would continue.

As I grew into a young woman, I learned how to slowly tan my body to a respectable color so I wouldn't be an outcast. Possibly I had some of Papa Brice's epidermis in my makeup and was thankful. Nowadays people stay out of the sun.. As I observe pasty pale specimens, I remember Papa Brice, who was always tan. He was golden until he took his last breath at age ninety eight.

I am thankful for the beach mentality that has always been part of my existence. Generations of "old salts." I know why Papa was drawn to his daily appointment with the ocean. He experienced all of the physical and emotional anticipation common to lovers of the sea.

My parents are in their eighties now. We still travel together to places we favor the most. We fly away in winter and follow the sun. My husband, sons and their wives shed their computers and layers of career burdens. Palm trees, the ocean roar, sand in our teeth and our sheets. A call from Daddy is all it takes. "Hello there, Daughter. Let's go where it's warm."

COUSINS

Aunt Wilma lived in a "slow" house. When my mama, daddy and I stepped inside her home, time slowed to a crawl. Through youthful eyes, I saw very old, black furniture and heard the loud ticking of a big clock on the mantel. Our shoes made sticky popping sounds on flowered linoleum floors. Tap water in jelly glasses was our refreshment. I drank the warm liquid while imagining sipping iced cold Coca Cola at Dillard's Drug Store where sun shone in the windows and bounced off of chrome stools.

Aunt Wilma had a coal stove in her bedroom. The whole atmosphere was stiffeling. Summers were better when everyone gathered on her screened-in front porch.

Every summer, Aunt Wilma's grandson, Childers Atchley, came to visit for a couple of weeks. Childers was accompanied by his parents, Virgil and Loretta. The Atchleys had moved north to Virginia when Childers was a baby. I guess that's why he talked a little funny. His words were rolled and rounded out. I tried talking like that but it didn't last long.

As I understand genealogy, Childers and I were third cousins. Each of us was an only child, so distant kin didn't mean much. Having someone in the family who was close to your age and willing to play with you was all that mattered. I always thought Childers was quite different from the kids I was accustomed to. For one thing, he was, at age ten, a walking encyclopedia. He didn't boast about the things he knew. I suppose he was just born smart and didn't know any difference.

Childers was smart but he was a bit clumsy. He had trouble riding a bike and his chubby hands fumbled when it was his turn to make a move in Monopoly. He talked about becoming a doctor. The mention of his life's goal sent my mother into restrained hysteria.

"Now, Childahs," she would say in a somewhat shakey southern drawl. "Ya not thinkin bout becomin uh surgeon are ya?!" "Why, we need all th gen-ral prak-tish-un-ahs we can get!"

I think my mama must have had nightmares where she was stretched out on an operating table with Childers standing over her. In the dream, he was probably wearing an oversized white mask to cover his nose and mouth. A nurse at his side, kneading his fat awkward hands into large rubber gloves. It was a pretty scary thought.

Childers was nice to the point of being downright annoying. When I asked, "Whatcha wanna do?" He always gave the same answer, "Anything is fine with me. Whatever you would like to do." He probably longed for a day at the library but he must have known my interests and limitations.

Loretta Atchley was attractive, petite, proper and nervous. Virgil was easy going and could slowly talk your ears off. Mama and Daddy said Virgil had a "big job" up in Virginia. I wasn't sure what that meant but it sounded good.

Childers, unlike me, obeyed his parents without question. Loretta pampered and babied him continuously. Childers was required to use nosedrops and wear socks to bed every night, winter and summer. I guess this was supposed to prevent every disease known to man, but the thought of sleeping in Aunt Wilma's stuffy house with socks on caused me claustrophobic paranoia. When Childers did grow up and become a doctor, I imagine he realized that his parents' "home preventative medicine" hadn't been such a good idea.

Virgle was kind of a regular guy. He showed Childers and me how to find rabbit tobacco in the woods and he introduced us to dried cornsilks. These gifts of nature could be rolled up in paper and smoked. I made many trips into the woods behind our house to gather the crunchy gray leaves until one slip ended it all.

I hid in the bathroom with my rolled up paper and positioned myself in front of the mirror so as to view my every sophisticated move. With a wooden match, I lit the stuffed cylinder. Red and yellow flames looked gigantic as they reflected and blazed out at me from the mirror.

I threw the cigarette toward the toilet where it persistently burned until the toilet seat became only a charred remain of it's former self. It was very hard to explain to my parents. I had to buy a new toilet seat with my allowance. Smoking just wasn't worth it.

Childers wasn't much of an outdoors boy and I wasn't much of in indoors girl. So we compromised. Childers went with me out to Aunt Wilma's backyard to look at the chickens. Childers was unsteady on a bicycle, but he rode with me anyway.

I stayed inside with Childers, played board games and listened to music. My cousin's appreciation for classical was foreign to me but we alternated between Beethoven and Buddy Holley.

We went to the Ellis Theater to see picture shows. Although our town was small, Childer's parents insisted on driving us to and from the theater. Once, after being emersed in a world of Roy Rogers, we walked out into the blinding daylight. After adjusting our eyes and watching the other kids walk toward their homes, we realized that no one was there to chauffeur us.

We waited, for what seemed to us, like an hour. Then, at my suggestion, we took off on foot toward Aunt Wilma's house.

When we were finally found, or rather "rescued," Loretta let us know, in no uncertain terms, that we should never have been so brazen as to walk the sidewalks and cross the streets of that town. It was purely a miracle that we were not kidnapped or dead in a ditch.

Summers came and went. Our periodic visits were unchanging and our relationship remained compatible. The ease of our friendship was due to Childer's nature, not mine.

In the summer of 1959, I was invited by Loretta to spend a week at the Atchley home in Virginia. Wow! I had never been far away from home all by myself. Mama and I made plans and packed ironed dresses, shorts and shirts. We knew that Loretta would have every minute planned and I had better have the right attire.

There I was, fourteen years old, planning to get on a train and end up in a totally unfamiliar place. The day before the trip, I cried from fear and excitement. Mama cried too.

The memories of that visit will stay with me always. Everything in their house was crisp and fresh.

My sheets, towels, the linen napkins and the very breeze that blew through opened windows. Loretta had every day planned down to the minute. Sightseeing, plays, swimming, educational tours. It was wonderful.

I found out that Childers had some "normal" friends. I never pictured him with real school friends. He had collected a stack of rock and roll 45 records and the two of us danced in the livingroom. We laughed and joked and dreaded the end of the week.

I felt very grown up, having ridden the train to Virginia and getting ready to ride it home. But the illusion of "adulthood" disappeared as the train whistled toward the south and home. My destination found me looking for that familiar hat and suit. I ran like a little girl, toward my daddy.

Childers and I didn't see each other much after that summer. I worked at Girl Scout camp and looked forward to college. I went to a state school and my cousin went to Harvard. I contacted Childers when Virgil died.

Dr. Atchley is a successful physician, but not a surgeon. His children are grown, as are mine.

We may never see each other again but for a time, our summers were enriched from being together and learning to accept each others differences. We needed to be surrogate siblings for a while, and dance through the awkward years.

INSIDE THE SHADOWS

Ricie was asleep. I had no idea what time it was, but it seemed late. Becky was sleeping soundly beside me in one of Ricie's creaky old beds. A siren was blaring but Becky continued to sleep. I shook my cousin who drowsily resisted. "Wake up, Becky! We gotta to go downstairs." She didn't understand my insistence, but finally complied.

Our bare feet tiptoed down the cool wooden stairs and stepped onto a rug which lay under the massive dining room table. In the dark, angles of street light and moonlight darted through windows. Luminous patterns which led us toward a sofa situated under the living room window. We climbed onto the cushions and folded our arms across the back of that ancient piece of furniture. Our small hands lifted the thick wide blinds and our eyes peered out.

Ricie's big white house was on the corner of a quiet street. Neighboring houses were neatly kept and surrounded by large trees. Those trees seemed to wave and beckon guests, just like the friendly people who lived there.

Diagonally across the street, a box-shaped, rock building looked even more severe at night. The building housed several offices, including the health department. I got my typhoid fever shot there every summer and was sick as a dog for days afterward.

A traffic light went from red to green. There were no yellow traffic lights in our town in the 1950s. You either stopped or went. My daddy was color blind and couldn't tell the difference between red and green. At some stops, the red light was on top and the green on bottom. At others, they were the opposite. Our street department must not have known upside down from right side up. There were no hoods over the lights in those days.

Daddy asked Mama to go all over town and write down the positions of the red and green lights that were situated in black compartments, dangling on cables. Daddy typed out the information and taped it to his car visor. He soon memorized the haphazard way our town had placed the lights. I felt sorry that Daddy couldn't see many colors but he seemed perfectly happy seeing yellow and murky blue. Guess he never knew any difference.

I sat beside Becky while we looked at the lights. She must have wondered why I had dragged her from a deep sleep to gaze out at nothing in particular. Our parents were out for a night of playing Bridge with their friends, and Ricie was babysitting.

Keeping children was not one of Ricie's favorite pastimes, but I think our daddies slipped her some money for the job, even though we were related. We weren't really babies at seven and eight, but we were too young to stay alone.

Of the two of us, I was the visible worry wart. I just knew my mama and daddy were involved in an accident and the screaming siren was an ambulance taking them to the hospital. I finally broke the silence and asked Becky if she every worried about her parents. She sleepily responded, " uh, maybe sometimes."

Becky had three sisters she fought with, and a bunch of dogs at her house. She tramped around the woods with her BB gun and preferred the company of boys to girls. She was a bonafide tomboy. Since we were cousins, she was forced to be around me at times. I adored her and wanted to be just like her. I could give her a pretty good run for her money when we wrestled on the floor. But I never knew anyone who could pull off being like Becky.

My cousin was cute, with just a few freckles on her nose and a golden tan in the summertime. I had too many freckles, in my opinion and I never got a very good tan. Once, when Becky and I went to the picture show together, the lady at the ticket counter asked if we were twins. I've never forgotten that, because my self esteem grew to new heights. I don't imagine Becky was as flattered as I was.

The two of us counted the seconds it took for the lights to change from red to green and back again. My worrying subsided and I grew tired. We ascended the stairs and crawled back into bed.

When the summer morning called to us, I didn't feel worried anymore. Daylight could fix things sometimes. But there were other times when even the day grew heavy on my heart. It came out of nowhere and my chest beat like the loud ticking of Aunt Wilma's clock. Colors around me changed and, unlike my daddy, I could see them. I could see them straight through my long shadow in the late afternoon.

I didn't have any sisters, like Becky did. No brothers either. So, I spent a lot of time lying on the floor, drawing pictures. That activity lifted my spirits and took my mind off of myself.

I can still feel the cold tile floor on my stomach and see my creations under the bright overhead light. My shadow is gone, my drawings become three dimensional and I am lost inside a world without fear.

Art kept me alive with curiosity and anticipation. During the school year, I was eager to go home and draw. On warm southern winter days, I headed for the woods behind our house or sat on our easily accessible roof. I hated school with a passion. Homework was a necessity but I had little discipline for scholarly requirements. I eked by with Bs and Cs.

Becky made all As. She knew about football, was great at math and popular with boys and girls. I compared myself to this cousin of mine and always came out on bottom.

I couldn't be like Becky, but I wanted to. At a very young age, I wondered where and how I would end up.

I never thought being able to draw was anything special. I never saw it as much of a talent. It had just always been there, like Daddy's color blindness. I couldn't do math, and having mathematical ability was what made a person smart, ready for college and the world beyond. At least, that's what my teachers seemed to think.

Sitting on the huge rock behind our house, I thought about everything a twelve year old could conjure up. Why did I worry so much? Why wasn't I smart and what would become of me if Mama and Daddy both died? Life can be tough in the deep recesses of a kid's mind.

I found out about Girl Scout camp from Becky and other girls who went there in the summers. I wanted to go, so my parents consented. I met girls who knew nothing about me. I made new friends. Our activities were so constant and strenuous that our raging hormones were left steaming on the trails.

Becky and I attended camp through our pre-teen and teenage years. But, we were in close proximity only once when we were assigned to the same cabin. I'm not sure if she revealed our relation or not. She had been going to the camp longer than I, and had her circle of friends.

One night, after "lights out," Becky and another girl talked long into the night. I listened, fascinated while I learned more about my cousin than I had ever known. She talked about her boyfriend, family life and a multitude of things that teenagers discuss.

I realized that Becky had concerns and worries of her own. I thought worries were exclusive to me. I thought Becky had it all. I couldn't see, like Daddy's color blindness, that she didn't. Not until that night in the cabin when sounds of frogs, katydids and other night creatures did not drown out that revelation.

I believe Becky and I were friends even if we weren't very verbal with each other. Friends come inside the shadows of our walls and help the darkness fade. They surround us, like Ricie's soft old creaky bed. They awaken, willing to share our fears, and help us see the difference between red and green.

MEMORIES IN A BOTTLE

Her eyes were wide open as she lay on the right side of the double bed. It was the side closest to the door, and her parents who were in the living room. They were watching a TV show.

At six years old, she was fretful and squirming. Unable to sleep, or not wanting to. She felt like she was missing out on something fun. She was bored with lying in bed and wanted to see what was on television. Her mind anticipated the next day. Play, discovery and friends in the neighborhood. Morning seemed terribly far away.

A light shone from the kitchen. Illumination bounced off of the linoleum floor and enamel table top. Her parents tip-toed around, trying not to disturb her. The house was small.

He stood in the doorway, his dark form backlit from the glare of the kitchen. He knew that she was still awake. Her daddy pulled a chair beside her bed and sat down. His presence comforted her.

"Having trouble sleeping, Honey?"

"I can't," she replied.

He touched her forehead and stroked her silky hair. He calmed her with his touch, and her eyes became a little heavy.

She saw something glisten in her daddy's hand. The glass object reflected light from the kitchen. He held her mother's perfume bottle. The top looked like a tiny crystal ball and had always fascinated her. The bottle of amber liquid from her Mama's dresser. It had been around for as long as she could remember. Sometimes she would gaze into the little ball, and wish that she could see into the future.

Her daddy's large blue eyes smiled right along with his mouth. She liked his face. It was young and round, with a mischievous look. He loved to tease and joke with his daughter.

"Sweet dreams for a sweet girl," he said.

He anointed her pillow with the rich aroma and sat with her a while. He told her a story about a princess who lived on a beautiful island. She became comfortable with the night as she sunk deep into fragrance and rest.

She was no longer a child, and sleep seemed unattainable. Her fifty-eight year old body twisted into and out of hot sheets. The cool breeze and low hum of the table fan did nothing to diminish her fever or thoughts. Restful sleep at her age was rare. Most nights were like that.

She longed for childhood with it's zest for life and painless body. She missed her daddy. She wanted to go back in time to the little bungalow with the big Magnolia tree out front.

Her bones ached with all forms of medical diagnoses. A nightly restraint. She took pills. Anything to ease the pain and get through the night. But medication didn't eliminate sorrow or dry the wet tears on her pillow.

Her husband stirred, and knew that she was having another bad night. The man who was always in tune with her joy and pain, quietly got up and walked around to her side of the bed. He massaged her shoulders, back and legs until tightness and tension released. Professional duties awaited him in the morning, but that didn't matter. He loved her and wanted her to have rest.

She awoke to the smell of coffee that he had made. Their big black dog nudged her face. He was a patient old hound and willing to sleep when she slept. But enough was enough and it was time to get up.

The air in the room felt unusually fresh. A faint aura floated across her senses. A memory, perhaps, or fragments from a dream? Her arthritic hand automatically reached for the bottle of pills. A familiar plastic form that held relief for daily motions.

She felt, instead, an object, smooth and cool to the touch. A slight chip on the rim did not alter it's beauty. A small, round glass top caught flickers from late morning sun. The container held amber liquid. The source of a forgotten fragrance.

A feeling of hope swept over her for the first time in years.

SONG FOR PAPA

The wind chimes outside my studio sound like distant church bells. Their tones are low and pleasing to my ears. Sounds of the waterfall nearby roll over the chimes and reach up to birds singing in the trees.

The music created outside of my screened door causes me to navigate toward the drawing board on one end of the room or the daybed on the other.

My husband's father made the wind chimes. Papa made them from scraps he found at the factory where he worked for years. Chimes that were created from noisy, clanging metal against metal became soothing melodies to the ears of his children.

Papa was close to retirement when I first met him. He looked youthful and handsome with his shock of white hair and tanned skin. He spent week-ends planting and working his large garden. A garden that was beautiful to look at and impeccably maintained.

The delicious, lush results were appreciated by every family member who stopped by. No one left without a full sack of Papa's intense efforts. Colorful rewards which were more than just food to enjoy. They were his gifts to us.

Papa was a gardener and a carpenter. It was amazing to see what one man could build with his own two hands. His greatest joy seemed to come from helping his children. He built a workshop for my husband and crafted easels for my artwork.

His delight was to be needed.

This father-in-law of mine was not in my life for very long. Not nearly long enough. I felt as though I was just getting to know him, to feel comfortable in asking his assistance.

I was learning to enter into conversation with this quiet yet exceptionally witty man. His life taught me not to wait too long. Not to wait until I'm unafraid to reach out.

I miss him. But I hear his voice and notice his mannerisms in my husband.

There is a vacant seat when Big Band music entertains us on summer evenings in the park. But my husband's smile is the same as his dad's and his feet tap to the music of Papa's era. And the wind chimes are playful on the breeze.

THE IVY STAYS GREEN

Ricie had that glassed-in porch at the back of her house. It kind of slanted down from years of settling. That's where she nursed her ferns, African Violets, Christmas Cactus and other varieties she knew the names of, but I didn't. It was cold out there but not so cold that the greenery didn't flourish.

She told me African violets do much better if they have other African Violets for company. So, I never saw one sitting alone. She had Violets lined up on her kitchen windowsill and placed around her light-filled bedroom. Her antique tables were ruined from water spilling over the pots, but she never even noticed. She loved her flowers more than her furniture.

In the grocery store, Ricie went straight to the plant section and spent a lot of time there. Then she bought a minimum of food supplies. Just enough to get her by for a few days. She hated to cook.

We both disliked winter. But she had a better attitude about it than I did. I never understood how she could get so happy just from sitting in a spot of sun in that house in the dead of winter. How a car ride on a freezing sunny day could lift her spirits as if it were July. And those Christmas Cactus blooming throughout the short days. They were a pretty sight, I'll have to admit.

Ivy was plentiful around Ricie's house. My husband and I dug some up, planted it at our new house and now it's about to take us over. We got almost all of our plants from my grandmother. She had everything! Anything you could possibly want.

It's nice, now because it's like we have some of the fruits of her handy work. Not to get sappy, but it's as if we have a part of her living with us. Ricie wasn't sappy, thank the Lord.

I was outside throwing the ball with Willoughby. Our dog is named after my great, great grandfather. Anyway, it was so bleak out there, it was enough to cause a psychotic reaction. I've been looking up at this one tree when I'm out there with my dog. I've watched it through all of the seasons and needless to say, it's nakedness has no appeal.

I look up at it and I pray and thank God for the seasons because I know that's what I'm supposed to do. And I know there's an order to things and we need to be thankful for all of it, and how everything works together. But I still want to move to Florida. I can thank the Lord for things down there.

We can't move to Florida right now. I know that. Eddie's got to retire and he's eight years younger than I am. I might be dead by then. Anyway, I was throwing the ball and looking up at that tree and thinking about Ricie. Then I noticed how the Ivy spills over the walls around the driveway and how it's just about everywhere on this plot of land where our house sits.

Lately, I've been spending a lot of time in the sunroom getting my "light therapy" as they refer to it these days. The sun pours into that room and I look at the palm plant I'm trying to care for through the winter. I think it might make it.

I know spring will eventually get here like it always does. Right now, I'm just going to go outside, throw the ball with Willoughby, and be glad that the ivy stays green.

SUNDAY SEASONS

Sundays were as predictable as rain in a thunderstorm. Summer Sundays were somewhat better than winter Sundays. But the motions that we went through on "the day of rest," were always the same.

Mama didn't cook a big breakfast on Sundays. We had cold cereal and toast. Daddy and I were late sleepers and didn't have time to stuff down a a lot of food before putting on our Sunday clothes.

I wiggled into a stiff, frilly dress, pulled on white socks and buckled my shoes. Sunday clothes were an indication of what the day would be like. Stiff. Stuffy and uncomfortable.

The styles changed as I grew older, but the clothes were always irritating and confining. Garter belts, stockings and jacket dresses replaced lacey attire, but the scratchiness remained. I wanted to feel the softness of my faded blue jeans. But "casual" church dress, was unheard of at that time in history.

The three of us slid into our long car, and shut the doors. Daddy backed out of the driveway and headed for Lester Memorial Methodist church. It was a short drive to the church, and I had the back seat to myself. But what was to come in the afternoon, put dread in my heart.

My mother gave me the same litany that I heard every Sunday. She named cousins and friends who "enjoyed church." Why couldn't I " be like the other children?" I always wondered how on earth she knew what the other children were thinking.

I'm not so sure that the "other children" liked church as much as my mother thought. I liked God. It wasn't that at all. I just didn't think He wanted me to suffer so much on Sundays.

I entered my Sunday school class and saw familiar faces. Most of the kids I went to school with, were either Baptists or Methodists. I was grown before I realized that going all the way through school with the same children, was a rare occurrence.

We had a variety of Sunday School teachers through the years. Mrs. Farmer was fat. She had dimples, rosy cheeks and a cheerful smile. But her positive attitude could grow as dark as a massive cloud. Mrs. Farmer transformed in an instant when some of the boys acted up. I have a clear memory of our teacher, heaving herself up from her seat, slowly crossing the room and slapping Timmy Chandler in the face. I don't remember anything that Mrs. Farmer taught us. I just remember her round face and her disciplinary actions.

During my preteen years, Mr. Whimple came on the Sunday School scene. He had been some big officer in the military, and he ran his class like a platoon. He yelled, "at ease!" and clapped his hands loudly. He must have been over six feet tall. He was lean and mean and we were terrified of him.

I don't remember Mr. Whimple's teachings, either. Just his amplified voice and his lanky movements.

Each year, we went through a "promotion ceremony." We received a certificate with a picture of Jesus surrounded by loving children. Our names were written out in fancy script, followed by the words, "promoted to the 'so and so' class." I never knew anyone who failed Sunday School. Not even Timmy Chandler.

On promotion Sundays, our parents treated us as if halos were floating above our heads. We really didn't do anything special to get "promoted." The Sunday school teachers were probably glad to see us move on.

By the time I reached Maggie Marsh Bailey's class, I felt quite grown up. Mrs. Bailey told us to call her, "Maggie Marsh," so that's what we did. I called all of the grownups in my parents' social circle by their first names, so it didn't seem unusual to me. We lived in a very small town, and addressing adults by their first names was an accepted practice.

I finally "heard" some teaching when I sat in Maggie Marsh's class. Sometimes Maggie Marsh's eyes would fill up with tears while she was talking. She'd get all choked up and the kids would cover their mouths to keep from laughing out loud. Later, I decided that I understood why Maggie Marsh cried so much. She was as confused and depressed by her teaching as I was. I learned that we were "born in sin." I couldn't understand how a little baby could be so sinful, so I came up with my own explanation that I shared with no one.

I had heard about sex from my classmates. I hadn't heard a thing about it from my parents. But I did know that it was the most disgusting sounding thing that had ever entered my ears. So, I concluded that if that's how babies got here, then they absolutely were "born in sin." Doing that repulsive act, HAD to be a sin.

So, I thought I understood about being "born in sin." But I never did like the idea of it. I wished that babies could get here by some other method.

We entered high school, and were placed under the theologically unsound leadership of Mr. Sandlin Rath. Mr. Rath was not in my parent's social circle, so I called him, Mr. Rath. He did not teach according to a lesson plan, or a particular book, or even the Bible.

Mr. Rath sat at a desk in front of us and rambled about everything from fishing the Warrior river to the importance of wearing clean underwear. He rambled and rambled. Mr. Rath didn't seem to mind if we giggled and asked stupid questions. We didn't seem to bother him at all. That man was an enigma, and I am thankful that he made going to Sunday school, interesting.

I began to look forward to church functions. Methodist ministers are transferred every three or four years. That can be good, or bad. But once, during my childhood, it was really good. The Reverend Bert Goodwin and his wife, Ella were sent to our church, and I began to look forward to going. They were youthful and vibrant and didn't carry around the "morose" attitude common to so many pastoral people. They took the youth group to Florida and participated in the fun. I began to see God in a whole new light.

Church balconies must have been built for teenagers. We sat together and paid no attention to sermons. We drew pictures on our bulletins and passed notes back and forth. We drifted off in our minds, and thought about an upcoming church hayride, or swimming with our friends at Highland Lake.

Sometimes, Mama put a roast in the oven before church, and we'd go home to eat. But more often, we raced the Baptists to the Gold Star Restaurant. Methodist ministers preached brief sermons, so we could get out early enough to continue our "fellowship" at the Gold Star.

There were some Sundays when I managed to escape the dreaded afternoon. I might be invited to go home with a friend, or join a crowd for a movie. But my memory holds the way that Sundays were most often played out in my family.

Winter Sundays were by far, the worst. I knew that I had school ahead of me the next day. That, in itself caused anxiety.

After Sunday dinner at the Gold Star, we headed up the mountain to our rather isolated home. I liked the little house downtown in between my grandmother and Aunt Annie. I wished we had never left it. Neighbors strolled by, and there was life on the streets and sidewalks there.

I enjoyed the woods that surrounded our new home, so I made friends with the trees and rock formations. But, I missed the activity surrounding the little house in town.

Daddy sat in his easy chair with the Sunday newspaper. I read the comics, then watched an old movie on TV.

I knew the pattern, and I knew it would never change. At three o'clock in the summers, earlier in the winters, Daddy would stand up in the middle of a circle of newspapers on the floor. He'd stretch, yawn and walk to the kitchen.

He reached for his favorite peanut butter glass, which looked something like a beer mug, and filled it with water from the kitchen sink. He drank a whole glass of tap water. I liked ice in my water, but Daddy didn't seem to care. The back of his left hand was perched on his hip while he drank the water and starred out of the kitchen window. He put the glass down on the counter, took a deep breath and said, "Ahhhh!" His utterance made that tepid water sound like it was the best thing he had ever tasted.

When I heard the, "Ahhhh," I knew it was time. The good part about it, was that I was allowed to wear my blue jeans and comfortable shirt. But there was no escaping what lay ahead.

The three of us got in the car and drove toward our first stop. My grandmother was waiting on her porch. She lived by the clock. She was regimented and punctual, and expected everyone else to be. If Daddy drove up three minutes "late," he heard about it. Mama got out of the car, let my grandmother slide in beside Daddy, got back in and shut the door.

My grandmother wore a bright blue coat. Underneath, she had on her Sunday finery, which was always tasteful and flattering to her blue eyes and brown-gray hair.

We drove less than half a block to Aunt Annie's house. Aunt Annie was my grandmother's sister, but was not rigid, when it came to the time of day. Sometimes, I'd get out of the car, walk up the steps onto Aunt Annie's small front porch and knock. She'd come out, smiling and happy.

When we lived next door to her, Aunt Annie let me sit at her kitchen table and eat sugar out of the bowl.

Daddy drove to the end of the block and took a left. Aunt Maude was another one of my grandmother's sisters. She was outside examining a barren winter bush in front of her house. She wore a drab, long winter coat and old-lady high-top shoes. Her hair was always pulled back into a thin bun on top of her head. She blended into the gray winter days.

Aunt Maude didn't smile or joke much. She was too religious to do that. She was "as good as gold," Mama said, but all I saw was misery.

Next, we were off to Aunt Flora's house. At this point, my lungs were starting to close up and panic was setting in. All of my aunts wore heavy coats, yet they were always cold. The smell of car heat mixed with moth balls caused a sickness that has scarred me for life.

My grandmother and three aunts were widows. Aunt Flora came smiling and lumbering out of her brick house. She was kind of square-shaped and wasn't very attractive. Her big black coat was square, and her face was square, but she had a pleasant personality. She entered the car, holding her jar of Vaseline. She rubbed Vaseline on her lips, across her false teeth and on her tongue. She said it was to keep her dry mouth from smacking so much. She must have had an awareness that most old people didn't have. I wished she had shared her Vaseline secret with all of the old people I knew.

My daddy was a saint to carry out this ritual every Sunday. Five women Daddy and I, packed like Sardines in a hot car on a cold afternoon. I always sat by the back window, and quietly turned the crank so that there was about a half-inch crack for air. I would stick my nose in the crack and try to satisfy my oxygen starvation. I do believe I would have died if it hadn't been for that small opening of air.

We drove out of town into the countryside. Winter scenery was bleak, even when the sun shone. Sometimes I felt like the sun was just too bright. It had a cold yellow sharpness to it, and gave me a headache.

Summer sun was warm yellow and splattered through lush green trees. The only time I liked winter was when a rare snowfall locked us into the mountain, school closed, and I could play in the powdery white for hours.

Curvy roads, excessive car heat, wool coats and five women talking at once, were enough to make me look forward to school on Mondays.

Occasionally, Daddy would stop the car and let me get out to look at horses in a field. I loved horses. I wanted to jump over the fence, hop on one of them, and race away.

Sunday drives were a year-round recreation for my parents and aunts. The summers were a little better. No heavy coats and more than a half-inch crack in my back window. But the old ladies didn't like a lot of air blowing on them. So, I just sat and hoped that Daddy would stop at the Dairy Queen for ice cream.

I'm not sure when "Casual Sundays" became a part of worship services around the country. But I surely was glad to see them in my life! No more stockings or itchy clothing. I wore soft, loose cotton dresses, and comfortable shoes. It made all of the difference to me. I just don't think the Lord meant for us to suffer so much in binding finery.

Sunday afternoons are different, now. My husband and I often come home from church, eat sandwiches and enjoyed afternoon projects. But, soon after I married Eddie, I found out that he enjoyed Sunday afternoon drives!

In the beginning, I pretended to share his enthusiasm for drives in the country. I'd sit in the passenger seat, and crack the window in winter. I'd close my eyes and try not to throw up while we followed snake-shaped curves, up and down hills.

On some of those Sunday drives, Eddie would play music from the seventies. I was having babies in the seventies, and when I did listen to the popular music, it affected me like morning sickness. The whole scenario was more than I could bear. But, I wanted the two of us to enjoy all of the same things.

How could I, a grown woman, have subjected myself to so much torture? It was no one's fault but my own. I had the "couldn't say no" syndrome, until one day, I had to confess.

I told my husband everything. My history of claustrophobic Sunday drives, and nightmares about a thousand relatives in big coats walking toward me, surrounding me, taking their coats off and piling them on top of me.

My husband had noticed that I looked rather green on our outings. He was understanding and we discovered that we had other things in common that were enjoyable.

It's not that I mind riding in a car. As long as I know a destination awaits me. Heading for the beach, shopping, or a camping trip. I must have the assurance that we will stop, and a vacation will be waiting for us at the end of the line. To me, There is a big difference between "a drive" and going somewhere.

THE BASIC "A"

The "basic A" had nothing to do with school when spring rains came. Educational facility doors would soon be locked and students scattered until September. Everyone's summer life was different. Mine had been dreamt about, looked forward to and anticipated while gazing out of drab winter windows.

"Basic A" is the beginning of a correctly laid out campfire. Three sticks in the shape of an, "A," create the starting point. Tinder is piled into the center of the A, then kindling then fuel. It all turns out looking like a tepee.

Years after my instruction, the aroma of woodsmoke causes excitement to well up in me. Flames in slow motion play themselves out like movies I never tire of.

The metal trunk was hoisted from a garage shelf and taken to my room. I unlocked the rusty latches, and opened the top to my one piece of camp luggage. Inside the deep compartment, an earthy flavor wafted through my nostrils and made me heady with past summer memories.

Thankfully, school dresses were put away. My tomboy persona emerged along with the musty trunk smell. Cheryl at the local beauty shop gave me a "pixie" haircut and I wore Dan's soft hand-me-down clothes. Flash light, toiletries, T- shirts, shorts, jeans, tennis shoes, flip flops, bathing suit and more. I never tired of accommodating the list that came in the mail.

Daddy loaded the car with six weeks worth of gear and drove for what seemed like hours. The road wound around and up, with the forest becomming dense and cool. Tucked into southern mountains and waiting to be populated, were the rustic buildings and sparkling waters of Girl Scout Camp Cottaquilla.

I kept a little book for writing down camp songs. After our evening meals, the long lodge porch became a hall for singing those harmonious tunes. American, African and European melodies that had been sung around the world for years. Rounds, pensive ballads and ridiculous lyrics sent ripples down my back and across the moonlit lake.

As a camper, I envied and admired the counselors who woke us up too early, gave us our orders and protected us from harm. They were mysterious and intriguing when they gave each other secret signals and sly smiles. Their knowledge of the outdoors made me wonder if they ever left.

Did they have lives outside that circle of mountains? I couldn't imagine them doing anything else. The hidden nature of those young women intensified my curiosity. I was anxious to pursue the rugged training which gave counselors their privledged positions.

We learned how to tie every knot known to man, to canoe in perfect sync with our partners and to chop massive amounts of wood. The heavy ax hit the logs and formed a "V." Our movements were choreographed and soon became second nature.

We hiked until our muscles ached and our feet burned. But at night when we cooked our meals over hot coals, we laughed and joked and told exaggerated stories. Our filthy shoes and damp socks were removed and we drenched ourselves in cool stream water. Bedrolls were placed on hard ground. Groans and laughter eventually faded into the night.

Two summers of the counselor-in-training program were primitive and rugged. At times, I wanted to be back home in my large bed with sheets that didn't feel damp and smell of mildew. To sink deep into endless sleep. I was sick of the wooden seat in the smelly outhouse or even worse, a hole dug in the woods on backpacking trips.

I wanted a hot shower. But when I turned off the water which had been cold and prickly on my skin, those longings for a different kind of comfort evaporated. I felt the night air on my towel wrapped body and looked up at the stars. I smelled binder's twine, the rough yellow cord used for lashing together a multitude of necessary objects. I brushed my teeth at the outside faucet. I had developed a liking for the taste of strong mineral water. Night sounds of owls, frogs and other creatures lulled me to sleep as I lay in one of four small iron beds. I remember the sounds, and the kerosene smell of our snuffed out lantern.

Some girls didn't like camp. They cried everyday until the camp director called their parents to pick them up. But those of us who became counselors and bonded with the whole outdoor experience didn't mind grit in our campfire stew and lizards in our cabins.

Our friendships were grounded in the soil at camp. We swore to keep in touch until we could see each other the next year. But there came a time when "next year" wasn't an option. College graduation awaited us, or a career or maybe even marriage. Life after camp would not be like camp.

I think about Mary Cat, Tyler, Pete and Sharon. I think about all of the "Cottaquilla girls. I've imagined running into one of them forty years later. I don't know where they live, or if their last names might have changed.

Do my former camper and counselor buddies remember me? Do they remember those sad "last nights?" and the last night of all? Do they remember, as I do, sitting around the lake on that final evening, watching the campfire floating in the middle of the water?

The tall, tepee shaped fire which had been laid on a wooden raft, began with the "basic A." It was a glorious fire that painted the magic of camp life as the breeze blew into it's flames.

The fire made it's own course around the lake. Flickering blue and gold lights captured faces. Mental photographs to take with me through life. We watched and sang, cried and hugged. And we said, "good-bye."

SMOOTH REFLECTIONS

I was just under five feet tall. Standing over the lavatory, I watched delicate colors meander in and through soapy water. The white porcelain bowl was filled with fresh smelling bubbles and floral ladies' handkerchiefs. My index finger swirled the fabric around as I created imaginary liquid pictures.

Every woman and girl folded handkerchiefs into their plastic purses. The closures on our pocketbooks were snapped and our necessities complete. These feminine accoutrements were given to us as presents, for birthdays or Christmas. Mama thought they were a requirement, so I left them in my purse to be soiled by pencils and sticky candy.

A fist full of handkerchiefs was rubbed against an open palm, and then alternated to the other hand. I had observed the routine when my Mama and her sister washed out scarves and underwear.

I repeated the process and gazed at my youthful face in the mirror. A clean mountain breeze greeted the window and blew my strawberry blonde bangs to one side. I thought about my "Buster Brown" haircut and how it didn't go with those frilly patterns of delicate colors.

Soap suds evaporated as rinse water disappeared down the drain. I held two corners and lifted the first handkerchief. Water poured from the gauzy piece of cloth.

My face was no longer visible as I placed pinks and blues onto the smooth surface of the medicine cabinet mirror. My small hands spread the square and pushed out air bubbles. The fanciful fabric clung to it's image like a magnet. It was a short cut. Ironed handkerchiefs without the ironing. The activity intrigued me. A child's entertainment.

Occasionally, the colorful material would loosen itself from the drying place, and float to the floor. But most of the time, I had the pleasure of pealing the stiff crisp cloths from their smooth surfaces and folding them into smaller squares. Ready for drawers and our purses later on.

I don't carry pretty handkerchiefs in my bag anymore. Mama still does. She gives them to me as gifts and I put them away.

I grab paper towels off of the roll and cry into them. I cover my face and cry tears of age and the wearing of life. I was happy when I spread handkerchiefs on the mirror to dry. And Daddy was in the next room.

PENNIES

The pennies that once rattled in our pockets were now flat and misshapen. They held such charm for us that we were willing to give up their monetary value just to be able to collect them. Images of Abraham Lincoln on one side and wheat on the other, were melted beyond recognition. One time, a preacher gave me one with The Lord's Prayer stamped into it in tiny letters I never could figure out how they did that.

Railroad tracks ran right through the middle of Notasulga, Alabama. That's where my cousins and I lined up our pennies on the tracks and waited for the train. A massive engine with it's powerful weight and speed would transform our coins. We stood on the bank while the deafening sound roared past us. We waved at the engineer, passengers and finally the caboose. The only sounds left were our feet trampling down the grassy hill to gather our prizes.

On one side of the railroad tracks stood my great-aunt Vivian's house. It was a sprawling place with a screened-in porch on the front and a large yard beyond for children to play among the massive oak trees. Aunt Vivian's son and his wife lived next door. Their son, Harris was a wiry boy with blonde curly hair and freckles across his nose. Harris had a baby sister named, Jean. That baby was so darn special that we weren't allowed near Harris' house because we "might wake Jean up."

At Aunt Vivian's, I shared a bed with my cousin, Carol. One morning when dawn rested on my eyelids, I awoke to find Harris, soundly sleeping in-between Carol and me. Harris always wanted to be somewhere besides his house. He especially wanted to be with his first-cousin, Carol. I knew I wasn't part of their tight connection, but that was ok. I was just glad to be in the midst of cousins and adventures.

Aunt Vivian was a character and her moods were unpredictable. We never knew when we would be the objects of her wrath. I had been feeling "left out," angry, or maybe a little homesick. I wrote to Mama, told her I wasn't having any fun and asked her to come get me. Aunt Vivian found the letter before I mailed it. My great-aunt was tall, and her presence dominated a room. She came toward me, waving my letter. The envelope and contents were torn into shreds and thrown on the floor, while she simultaneously reprimanded me. I picked up the pieces of shredded paper and nothing more was said about the incident. I enjoyed the remainder of my stay.

On the other side of the railroad tracks, lived one of Aunt Vivian's sisters, Aunt Willie Lee. She and her husband owned an immaculate house with thick green squeaky grass that felt like a carpet had been placed outside. Her rooms were bright, airy and clean. Aunt Willie Lee was so sweet that it seemed as if honey slowly poured out of her deep southern drawl. Her cheeks were as rosy as the polished clay tile floor on the sun porch. She thought all of us were little angels. She would have never considered that we schemed, sneaked and were mischievous tricksters. I wonder if my mother and her cousins saw us as miniature imitations of themselves at our ages.

Aunt Willie Lee was married to Mr. Hope and, "Mistah Hope," is what she called him. I thought this was strange. Didn't she know him very well? Their children were the ages of my parents. Our Uncle Hope was dapper and handsome in his suit and hat. He walked the one block from his house to work every day of the week.

Our time in Notasulga gave us days that were stretched out and open to wherever our imaginations would take us. We had hideouts, secret codes and signs, cats, dogs, and a junk house filled with "costumes" for whoever we wanted to be. We meandered back and forth across the tracks sampling fresh summer vegetables and rich desserts.

Harris' daddy, Ed Reynolds was a true southern lawyer. My mother's side of the family bred lawyers, politicians, fishermen and a wide variety of opinions. When the whole bunch of them gathered on the porch at night, you could hear the laughing and storytelling echoing down the railroad tracks to meet the next oncoming train.

I can still see that small town in my mind's eye. It is as clear to me as a blue sky that goes on forever. The cousins are standing together with pennies lined up on the railroad tracks. We wait for the train's intense weight and heat to mold them into something more interesting. As I see reflections bouncing from the bronze objects that used to be money, I realize that like our lives, these transformations will never go back to being what they were before.

HUMDINGER'S SIDE

Mae and Humdinger lived in Birmingham, Alabama. The big city was about an hour's drive from my small hometown. Mama, Daddy and I would make the trip, about once a week, and spend the day. Daddy drove our 1950's Buick, with Mama beside him. I'd sit or lie down in the back seat. The drive always seemed long and boring to me.

When we entered the downtown part of Birmingham, tall buildings looked down on us and formed shadows as dark as our black car. The city was surrounded by a suffocating fog of burning rubber and emissions from the steel mill. Putrid air left me feeling sick. But I always looked forward to seeing Mae and Humdinger.

My mother's parents were opposite in nature and physical appearance. Mae was short and round. She had smooth olive skin, and thick wavy gray or purple hair. Her hair color was dependent upon whoever was available at the beauty shop. Mae's cheeks were always flushed from cooking and cleaning. But on top of the natural glow, she added round splotches of rouge. The red rouge was uneven, and caked around her hairline. She huffed, puffed and "perspired," while she scurried around and stooped to pick up lint off of the floor.

Mae had a sharp tongue. She was either abrasive or witty. We never knew which was coming. She alternately criticized and bragged on every member of her family. She justified her behavior by making references to her Irish heritage.

My grandfather's name was, Van Berry. No middle name. But, his granddaddy name was a mouthful. I think my cousin, Donald named him, "Humdinger," but I'm not really sure why. That's just who he was.

Humdinger was easy going in his demeanor and gestures. He was tall and lanky, moved slowly and was almost graceful in a manly sort of way. He had a mellow deep southern voice and his sentences were interrupted by long, slow swallows. It was as if the syrupy sound of his voice had to make it's way down into a tunnel and back up again. He was a quiet ship in a raging sea of women.

My grandfather knew that I was reprimanded by the women in the family, because he never stopped telling me, "Janet, I'm on your side." He made me feel special. He told me tall tales and jokes while he intently and tirelessly washed and waxed his green Plymouth. I thought that car was fabulous. Humdinger could spend an entire day making it sparkle, shine and smell like new.

Mae and Humdinger lived in a small apartment. Their lives were forever altered when Mama's sister, Vivian and her two children moved in with them. Vivian's husband, Bill left her. He didn't just leave Vivian, he left his children, too. My first cousins, Betty Anne and Donald were young, but Bill didn't care.

Mama and Mae were embarrassed over Vivian's divorce. No one got divorced in the 1950's. But it wasn't Vivian's choice. Her husband, Bill left her for Millie.

Years after retiring from being a Pharmacist, Humdinger got a job taking up tickets at a movie theater.

I saw him after his first day at work. He had on a white suit and he practically flew up the stairs. He said he felt "like a new man." And he made reference to wanting to work eight days a week. He needed is space.

Don was seven and I was six, when he told me why his daddy ran off with Millie. He said, it was because she had big bosoms. It was as simple as that. But it really wasn't simple at all.

As a very young child, Donald was put on a train in Birmingham, cared for by a transit employee and taken to his dad in Virginia. What goes through the mind of a child alone on a train at night? What fear and loneliness capture the crevices of his heart?

Betty Anne was ten years older than Don and she had made her decision concerning her father. She never got on the train, never went to Virginia in the summers. She spent her time with Vivian, Mae and Humdinger.

I adored my cousin, Donald. He was the brother I never had, and I followed him everywhere. At times he would get tired of me and chase me off. But, at other times, he allowed me into his secret world.

The apartment building was set on a small plot of land with very little play area around it. Across the busy street were more apartments, a nursing school, grocery store, dry cleaners and other businesses. It was all just an extension of the city which became bigger and bigger as we drove down the hill. But children have the ability to create what they need.

Beneath the apartments was a large basement for storage. It looked like jail cells, with bars dividing each tenant's space. Don had his very own key to the fat lock that secured the area. He built things and concocted potions in jars. The whole place was cool and dark, with an air of mystery. It was my cousin's private place, and I was much older when I realized how much he needed it.

My Aunt, Vivian, taught school. Everyday, during the school months, she went to work, came home, ate Mae's cooking, graded papers and went to bed. I thought Vivian needed to find another husband, but as far as I knew, she never had a date.

Aunt Vivian stayed mad a lot. She fussed at her children and she fussed at me. I didn't use proper grammar, so she took it upon herself to correct my every utterance.

Vivian must have spent her weekends buying brown dresses, because her closet was full of them. Her hair was reddish brown and she had a freckled, ruddy complexion. Sometimes, when I looked at her, all I saw was brown from her head down to her shoes.

But, there was a lighter side to my aunt. When I spent an occasional weekend at the apartment, Vivian would wake me up in the middle of the night to eat ice cream. When the two of us sat there in Mae's small kitchen while everyone slept, she was witty and fun. Dewy cream on her face gave her a youthful look and her freckles showed through. We laughed and talked under the bare overhead light. And I noticed she wasn't wearing brown pajamas.

Vivian, Betty Anne and Don had to sleep in one room. When Don was around eleven, he became sick and tired of sleeping in the twin bed beside his mother and sister. The only place for him to go, was the sun parlor, a very small windowed area off of the living room. But at least he could close the door and sort of be by himself.

Sometimes at night, when I would lie on the twin bed that used to be Donald's, I'd feel misplaced and far away. I was aware of the ubiquitous smells of moth balls, face powder, soap and rust. It was impossible to keep steel mill odors from seeping into cracks. Shadows created by street lights, pierced through the slats of large Venetian blinds. Train whistles and traffic made me feel empty and sad. At my own house, the air smelled fresh, and I could hear Katydids through open windows.

I don't know what it was about that city that made me feel sad at such a young age. The feeling still accompanies me when I pass through Birmingham. I was lonely when I was with my relatives. Now, I feel lonely because they aren't there anymore. It might not have been the city at all. It could have been the layers, complexities and undercurrents of a family.

Mae and Humdinger had no time to themselves in their later years. Vivian was bitter, but never stopped loving the man who left her for a woman's outward appearance. Betty Anne didn't have a room of her own. She never complained. But once, I saw her lying on the bed, crying. Small quiet sobs.

Mama and her sister didn't get along with each other. Vivian was envious of Mama. Mama thought Vivian spent too much money on herself, and didn't help Mae and Humdinger enough. They fought constantly, and their love-hate relationship affected all of us.

My mother thought Betty Anne could do no wrong and constantly compared me to her. "Why can't you be more like Betty Anne?" Those words ring in my ears to this day. I wasn't anything like my first cousin and I knew that I would never measure up. I just wasn't motivated to try.

When Don was a teenager, he took a baseball bat and with every bit of rage he had in him, destroyed a bed at his dad's house in Virginia.

Millie was in her seventies when she committed suicide. She had a fatal disease and decided she couldn't live with it any longer. So, she turned on the car ignition and closed the garage door.

Vivian felt a ray of hope. She would have taken Bill back in a heartbeat. I never understood why she held onto a dream for so long. But, she began to look wonderful and youthful, until the day she received news that Bill had married his second cousin.

Rains were coming in torrents. Tornado warnings had been issued for the city, but Vivian ignored the storms. She also ignored the fact that she should not ride with her friend who was slipping into dementia.

When Greta drove up, Vivian entered the passenger side of the automobile and made a conscious decision not to buckle her seatbelt. Vivian died several weeks after the crash. A death wish? I don't know. None of us will ever know.

Although Don's law degree earned him a fairly safe position in Viet Nam, he volunteered for combat duty. He crawled on his belly in the swamps and slept in foxholes. He could have sat at a desk during his two year tour of duty, but he wanted to put himself in danger. He fought with the enemy, and every Vietnamese looked like the brokenness that lay deep within his heart.

Don married after the war. He was a good husband and father, thanks to the example he had in

Humdinger. But he wasn't able to keep the promise he made to himself in childhood. His commitment to family life was not to be carried out. Don, also, left his family when his son and daughter were very young, but not in the same way that his own father left his children.

Donald William Davis, was walking with his co-workers in a south Alabama town, when he collapsed on the sidewalk. My first cousin, my big brother-hero, died of a massive heart attack at age, forty-one.

Each one of Betty Anne's three adult children are mentally ill. Once again, she is trapped. "Never a room of her own." Betty Anne has never been free.

Like most every family, this one was complex. The memories are good and bad. Some are confusing, and some are blocked out forever.

But I'll always be able to hear Humdinger's calm voice and his contagious laughter. He was happy and uncomplicated. He surrounded me with ease and acceptance. He didn't seem to mind his female-dominated household.

My granddaddy stretched out those lanky arms to all of us. I know now, that I wasn't the only one. Humdinger was on everyone's side.

EPHIE'S IDEA

"Tutor!? No way! I can't do it, and believe you, me, Eddie can't do it either. You've got me down here going through clothes and stacking up canned goods because I can't even answer a telephone with two lines. I can't keep books and I can't file. People should do what they're good at and I am NOT a tutor."

Ephie looked down at me. She was tall and as black as a window you can't see out of at night. She and her husband, Rodney were in charge of the Neighborhood Christian Center. It did not matter how old you were, if you were a volunteer, you did what Ephie said.

"I'm tellin' you, you don't have to know math or nothin' like that ta tutor lil kids. Juz go down ta th church once uh week an listen ta them read. You don't have ta be some kinda genius ta do that!"

Rodney and Ephie were as different as night and some other night. He was smooth, quiet, eloquent and psychologically convincing. In one week, my husband, Eddie and I had signed up for the tutoring program of the Neighborhood Christian Center.

At least thirty children were standing up and singing to the top of their lungs. Scott and Jennifer headed up the program. They were a young couple who could have easily passed for Ken and Barbie. Their alabaster skin and blonde hair stood out in sharp contrast to Ephie, Rodney and the children who had never heard

74

"white church songs." But it didn't matter. Short, dark kids with shiny hair, focused on Jennifer's beauty and delicate directions that she choreographed with elongated porcelain arms and hands.

We were assigned to two sisters and their brother. Eddie took Whitney and Brandon. I took Nobie. The three Harris children were obviously genetically connected. They looked exactly alike. Although Whitney and Nobie could have passed for twins, they were a year apart. Ages five and six. Brandon was eight. Their six brown eyes were like none I had ever gazed upon. Large, soft and welcoming.

Tutoring wasn't nearly as bad as we had expected. Eddie and I could follow Kindergarten and grade school books. After an hour long session of reading and getting to know each other, we joined the kids in hot dogs and potato chips.

The children filed out of the building and stepped inside the rambling bus to be dropped off at their respective residences.

Weeks passed and the "Tutoring Program" became more comfortable. We were encouraged to form relationships with our charges. Ephie explained the importance of getting to know parents, taking the children on outings and developing bonds that went beyond the tutoring walls.

Within weeks, we discovered that Whitney, Nobie and Brandon lived in an immaculate little brick house with their siblings, mother and father. We found out that a family of stair-step children included, not only the three we had become familiar with, but also, Shaneka and Tamika. All five of them looked just alike! They had their mother's smile. Perfect teeth and an obvious love for food.

Shaneka was a little older and involved in basketball and other school activities, so she didn't join our group at that point. But, the minute we met Tamika, we knew we had acquired another family member.

Quita lived next door and Sherrell lived down the street. Two adorable little girls who were also in the tutoring program. Cousins and young friends got wind of our picnics, trips to the park, mall and movies. We had plenty of room in our van so we adopted the philosophy of "The more the merrier." We were becoming part of a neighborhood and part of a future that we couldn't begin to imagine at that time.

By the time Whitney and Nobie were in the third and fourth grades, Eddie and I were lost. We could not do the math and we couldn't do the English. Brandon was struggling and another volunteer began to work with him. We were becoming tired with the repetition of once a week meetings and we felt that we weren't offering much in the way of helping with school work. It was time for us to move on.

Brandon was growing up and getting a little tired of being the only boy in our group. He and his dad took off on fishing trips and he left the girls to their activities with Eddie and me.

It was time to move on from tutoring, but not the families we had "adopted." We started our own brand of "teaching sessions" and they didn't include book learning. We talked to the girls about lots of things. We occasionally had to reprimand the children and teach them lessons about not getting everything they wanted at the mall. Nobie was the pouter. She would stomp around and stick her lip out until we gave her an ultimatum.

Keeping up with four to eight little girls was quite a task. We were constantly counting heads, especially when we went to the park. They would fly in every direction.

After three years, Eddie and I had gained the trust of parents and guardians. We had spend-the-night parties at our house and trips to hear music in the park. We played games and doled out tons of junk food. We comforted scared children in the night who weren't used to a hillside, woodsy residence with an upstairs bedroom. The wind blew and trees brushed the roof. Kids ran downstairs screaming into our bedroom. But it was all worth it.

The first time Whitney and Nobie referred to us as their "Godparents," I was touched beyond belief. Black and White traditions in the south are similar, but sometimes the differences are a bit confusing. At first, I assumed they meant "Fairy Godparents." But that wasn't it at all. We were seriously and forever initiated into their family. We were special, it had been decided and that was that. We now have about seven Godchildren. Almost an entire neighborhood.

Shanika is in college, studying to be in the medical field. Tameka went to Job Corp and is a caretaker for an elderly woman. She has her own apartment and a good future ahead of her.

Brandon worked all summer so he could buy a vintage car. He has a different girlfriend every week and he's all grown up. But he still hugs me and gives Eddie that "manly hand clasp thing." He's going to make it.

Whitney and Nobie are in high school. They call me every week and if I don't hear from them, I dial their number. Nobie, especially has become my young friend. She calls to tell me about her good report card and about "getting a new cell phone." I look forward to those chats that bring us closer together.

All of the neighborhood girls have lost interest in "music in the park." Playground equipment has lost it's appeal. But we still have spend-the-night parties and go to the mall. They are growing up and don't have to be watched anymore. When we go shopping, we take our walkie-talkies so we can check in often.

Eddie and I feel as if we're going to have to face the "empty nest syndrome" for the second time in our lives, like we did when our sons left home. Sherell, Quita, Ty and Megan are still in their earyl teens, so maybe they'll hang around us a while longer.

The Harrises have the cutest little niece. She's about five years old and is blessed with those big brown "Harris eyes" that can melt an iceberg. She's already started joining us on occasional outings when the older girls are willing to put up with her. "Shay Shay" has a little friend she likes to play with too.

Sometimes, in the afternoons, I drive over to the Harris' house to see Whitney, Nobie, their mother, Karen, and anybody else who might be around. Lately I've been noticing two little golden-colored sisters who look like they could be twins. They stand outside as if they're waiting for me. They hang on the tree swing and tell me about themselves. They draw me in and I think about "music in the park." I think about continuing the tradition and gathering up little ones.

Nobie just rolls her eyes and says, In her very protective manner, "Don't even fool wit dem, Janet, they gonna worry you ta death!"

BREAKDOWN IN GEORGIA

We had to get over to Georgia in a hurry. Uncle Monroe called mama, and asked her to come as soon as possible. It's a good thing Monroe had four sisters, because it seemed like he was always having a crisis.

I wanted to go so I could play with my cousin, Monroe, Junior. Mama didn't have anyone to leave me with. Daddy had to work and I was not going to stay with my sister. She was fourteen and the boss of the world.

So, Mama packed our bags and we went down to the train station. The Birmingham train terminal was huge and beautiful. The high glass dome ceiling spilled rainbows of light all over the black and white tile floor. There were wooden benches lined up for what seemed like blocks. People were rushing everywhere. It was thrilling to me, but Mama was sweating and wiping her round face with a handkerchief.

"Hurry up, Anne! "Don't bother that child, you can play with Monroe Junior when we get there. Get your hands off that filthy floor! Come on, we're gon miss our train!"

The trains were loud and I didn't like to hear metal screaming against metal. I covered up my ears until it was time to board. The porter took our bags and helped Mama up the steps to the train. Mama was a little heavy set.

It felt good to find our seats and lean back. I was too short for my head to rest on the crisp white linen that was draped across the back of the seat. So I lifted mine off and placed it under my head. After the train pulled out and finally picked up speed, the conductor came down the isles calling, "Tickets please! Tickets please!" He looked very important in his uniform and hat.

It was late in the day when we arrived in Winder, Georgia. Uncle Monroe was there to pick us up. Monroe Junior was along, too, because Monroe and I were best friends. We were the same age and I thought he knew everything. I knew he could "get into" everything, but that didn't bother me. I had a sneaking suspicion Monroe Junior was part of the reason we were in Winder Georgia and on our way to Aunt Florie and Uncle Monroe's house.

Aunt Florie was sick in the bed with another nervous breakdown. My mama had to help out. Mama could cook like nobody's business and she didn't mind washing clothes and cleaning up. I think Mama felt good when she was accomplishing things and helping people. Aunt Florie stayed in the bed with piles of tissues beside her. Sometimes I'd hear her voice through the closed door. "Oh, Lord, why me? Can't you help me?" And then she would go to sobbing. Mama went in there to pat her hand and take cups of hot tea.

My first cousin, Monroe Junior and I were seven years old that summer of Aunt Florie's nervous breakdown. Monroe's hair was a mass of curls and he had freckles all over his face. He was always getting into trouble and causing his parents distress. "Grief" was the word Aunt Florie used but I didn‘t understand what that meant. I don't think Monroe intended to get in trouble. I just think he liked to have a lot of fun. He was a boy with an adventuresome spirit and wild imagination.

We stayed outside most of the time while Aunt Florie was in bed, Uncle Monroe was at work and Mama was inside trying to make things better.

There were chickens out in the yard and a variety of dogs and cats. Monroe and I rode bicycles and pulled each other in a wagon. We walked down the street to play with other children, bought candy at a little fruit stand and climbed trees. Monroe helped me climb up so high in the branches that we could see what all the neighbors were doing. We were spies, cowboys and Indians.

Mama called us in for dinner and supper, but except for those times, we weren't allowed in the house. And we certainly weren't allowed near Aunt Florie. I asked Monroe if he was worried about his mama. He said, "Naw. she gets like that in the summer as soon as school lets out. She'll get well."

When it was bedtime, we had to be extremely quiet. We took our baths, got in our pajamas, tiptoed around and whispered. We made up signals with flashlights and flashed code from one end of the hall to the other. By eight-thirty, Monroe Junior went to his room and I climbed in bed in my room.

Monroe and I got up early in the mornings. I guess it was because I knew he was there and he knew I was there. We were happy about having each other to play with. Monroe never ran out of ideas. We always had something going on because, as Mama said, "Monroe Junior had an inventive mind." I wished I had an inventive mind, but I didn't. I just left the playing ideas up to Monroe. One day, Monroe had a terrific idea. But it turned out to be our undoing.

Mama had cooked breakfast for us, then she took Aunt Florie's meal to her on a tray. Beside the orange juice glass were two white pills. I figured they were for whatever Aunt Florie had. Mama washed the dishes, cleaned up the kitchen, poured herself a glass of ice water, picked up a magazine and went out on the side porch. Uncle Monroe was at work.

"Hey, Anne, I'm gonna make something that'll be more fun than a ride at the fair." I could hardly wait. I followed Monroe into the storage shack. There was so much good stuff in there. Hanging on a nail was a circle of rope. Monroe stood on a wooden box and took the rope down. It was wound up thick and tight. Monroe had an idea.

We walked up the back steps that led into the mudroom, which led into the kitchen. The refrigerator was to the right as you walked into the kitchen. Monroe carefully tied the rope to the refrigerator door. He made several knots and pulled on the rope to make sure it wouldn't come loose. He pulled the rope around the door facing, unwound the heavy circle and carried the remaining length outside.

Monroe walked across the yard, climbed up wooden slats that had been nailed to a large tree and tied the rope to a limb. Monroe's idea was that we could slide on that rope all the way from the mudroom to the tree. We'd be "Tarzan and Jane." It was going to be great.

I held the screen door open while Monroe took a running leap and grabbed onto the rope. I am an old woman now, but the sound of an earthquake in Winder,

Georgia still echoes in my mind. Those resting pills Aunt Florie took must not have worked too well, because she screamed bloody murder.

When Mama got to the kitchen, I saw that water had spilled all down the front of her dress. She was hollering and crying out for my daddy. Daddy was back in Birmingham, Alabama at work. Didn't she know that? I was still holding the screen door open. What I saw was going to result in Monroe and me getting severely beaten.

I couldn't move from my position. I was stuck and everything was kind of blurry. Dogs and cats were running in the house. The refrigerator was turned over on it's side on the floor and every piece of food at the Wise house was being lapped up by animals.

Mama's delicious roast, shelled peas, bread, eggs, milk, syrup, everything was on the floor. Glass jars were rolling in every direction and some of them were shattered.

Aunt Florie, who had not gotten out of bed even once while we were there, was standing in the doorway. Then she fainted dead away, on the floor. Mama's face was as red as fire. She stomped over to me and grabbed my shoulders. "You jus bettah get away from me, Alice Anne Berry. They-ah is no tellin whut I'm liable ta do!"

I ran up to my room and looked out of the window down onto the back yard. Monroe was gone. Monroe was gone far away, and I knew it.

First Mama called her brother at work and then she called Doctor Jenkins. Mama had managed to put a wet towel on Aunt Florie's head, fan her face and call out her name. Aunt Florie finally came to and immediately started babbling and shaking. Doctor Jenkins came by and gave Aunt Florie a shot.

Some of the neighbor men came over and helped get the refrigerator up off of the kitchen floor. They stood it upright and it seemed to still be working. Mama and Uncle Monroe mopped and cleaned up all the mess. Monroe Junior still hadn't come home. I missed my cousin something awful and I was mad at him at the same time. He left me to take all the blame. I knew the beating was coming. I just wished Mama would get it over with.

Around eight o' clock, I heard something outside my bedroom window. Monroe had climbed from a tree onto the roof and was crouched down under the window sill. "Anne! Anne!" he whispered loudly to me.

"Monroe Wise you get yourself in this house right now!" I told him with an assertiveness that surprised me.

I didn't know that Mama and Uncle Monroe were standing right behind me hearing every word. Uncle Monroe was going to kill his son and Mama was going to kill me. But Mama stood there and laid the law down to her brother.

My fever cooled and my heart slowed down as I heard the sweetest words that had ever come out of my mother's mouth. "Now, Monroe, you are not going ta whip Monroe Junior. I'm not gon whip Anne, and you're not gonna whip Monroe. We'll just forget about the whole thing. Monroe about scared himself to death anyway. Let that boy inside."

TRUE BLUE FRIENDS

Beatrice had wrapped the freshly cooked roast beef in tin foil and was gently setting her famous chocolate cake in a round metal box. Brown paper bags were filled with large red tomatoes, purple hull peas, and other spoils from the garden. Beatrice was my great-Aunt Amelia's housekeeper, cook and dear friend. She had been with the family since Amelia's children were small.

Amelia seemed awfully dressed up for a hot summer day, but she was making her monthly trip to see Doris and Paul. A dress and hat seemed appropriate attire for almost any occasion in the 1940's.

Coburn University was about a forty minute drive from the very small southern town of Slaton. Amelia's husband, Uncle Harry, was not interested in spending a weekend in a cramped little apartment with more people than square inches. Besides, their daughter, Doris was a newlywed, she and her husband were in school, and the whole idea was just too much of an intrusion. It intruded upon their privacy and it intruded upon his golf game with his friends in Slaton. Uncle Harry loved Doris, but a day trip now and then was enough for him.

Amelia was perspiring and fidgity in the hot kitchen. The redolence of yeast mingled with roast beef, chocolate and dirt from fresh garden vegetables. Aunt Amelia's house always smelled like that, even when she wasn't taking food to her daughter and son-in-law. She and Beatrice could really put on a spread.

The rolls had risen in the oven and were a golden brown on top. Beatrice placed them on a large plate and covered them with a dishcloth. Her shiny black arms were loaded with goods as she followed Amelia to the car.

It was a bit awkward for Aunt Amelia to get her stately body and large hat into the car. The straw hat with colorful flowers, bumped against the door frame and tilted to one side. Amelia looked at herself in the rearview mirror and straightened the hat. She pulled tissues out of her pocketbook and wiped excess rouge off of her cheeks.

Uncle Harry walked out of the house. He placed his freckled hands on the ledge of the open car window and told his wife to keep her mind on the road. They shared a brief peck of a kiss. Amelia waved at Beatrice and headed down toward Coburn.

Amelia spent her driving time thinking about her children's situations. She thought about her sons and her grandchildren. She didn't just "think" about her family, she constructed ways to work out all of their problems. She just knew if they did things her way everything would be fine.

Doris had told her mother that their next-door neighbors weren't very friendly. "Oh, what a perfect time in life to make friends with young couples and socialize. Spend time at each others apartments, cooking and playing cards." It was such a shame that Doris didn't make more of an effort to get to know those people. Amelia thought that Doris and Paul studied too much. They needed to get out more.

Amelia's mind was a book, and listening to her own thoughts made the trip go by quickly. She pulled the car up in front of the little apartment, got out and knocked on the door. No one answered, so she dug in her pocketbook for the key Doris had given her.

"Yoo hoo! Anybody home?" The apartment was a mess! A clothesline was strung the length of the livingroom and was filled from one end to the other. Amelia stooped to walk under the dripping clothes, went into the kitchen and out the back door. Amelia placed her hands on her large hips and looked around. She took a handkerchief out of her pocket and wiped her red face.

Amelia called, "Doris?!" and a young woman emerged from the apartment next door. "Uh, Oh, why, hello thay-uh. You must be my dautah's nay-buh." "Yes, Mam" the girl said. "I'm Jean Ellis and this is my husband, Bill." A tall blonde boy appeared at the back doorway. The youthful husband and wife walked out onto the grass to join Amelia.

Amelia noticed that they were both smiling and laughing in a delightful manner. They were absolutely delirious with joy. These couldn't be the neighbors Doris had told her about, thought Amelia. They were talkative and animated. Oh, how she did wish Doris and Paul would get to know this darling couple.

Amelia bid the two, "goodbye" and told them she hoped to see them again. She opened the back door and entered the kitchen. Oh, she needed to get that food inside before it ruined! But by the time Ameila had one foot inside the door, Doris greeted her mother with a big hug. Doris stepped back and took a good look at her large mother. She gasped, but before she

could say a word, her very southern mother began to
expound on the attributes and genuine friendliness of
Doris' neighbors. "Oh, Dah-riss, they wuh su friendly
an dahlin! Why, they just laughed an cay-rid on like
thay had known me all uv tha-uh lives!"

Doris waited. She looked up at the floral adorn-
ment on her mother's head and asked, "Mama, how
did my blue underpants end up on your hat?

BACKTRACKS

So what do I do in the meantime, between the past and now?

Spiritual wisdom says, Live in the present, savor the moment, don't look back. Let the future take care of itself."

But I look back and desire to relive an ordinary day. A day with intent and purpose. A day for stretching out hours and knowing each moment as never before.

In my imagination or in my dreams, I will live out this day.

I get up on a summer morning, drink fresh squeezed orange juice and grab a piece of bacon that Mama drained on a paper towel. Then I run barefoot to the sandbox. Squish my feet into the grainy texture cooled overnight and damp from the dew.

The metal sand pail is slightly rusty, but I look at the colorful pictures on it. I turn the pail around and around and watch the scenes repeat themselves like a movie. I look at the painting of the girl on the bucket. She holds a bucket and the girl on her bucket holds a bucket. I wonder how deep into the picture I can go.

I fill the sand pail full of gray-brown gritty particles, pat them down with my shovel and turn the bucket over to make an upside down impression of itself.

I know that I am six years old and right there in the sandbox that Daddy built. I feel the middle ground between my grandmother's house and my own little home and I anchor myself to it's safety.

Then I wander over to Ricie's big house and run up and down her stairs. I look out windows as high as a tree house. The Hickory trees are level with the windows and blow a breeze in my face. I feel like I'm flying.

Ricie is in the kitchen, stirring around, clomping in her "old lady" shoes. Then she sits at the kitchen table with a bowl of peas to be shelled. She playfully says, "You're a mess, Miss Janet!"

I stop in the living room and bang on her piano, slam the heavy black screened door and go back to my sandbox under the gigantic shade tree. Right that minute, I feel the freedom of climbing onto my swing and pushing myself so high that my toes touch negative spaces of blue sky formed by leaf shapes and clouds.

My friend, Anita comes by and we eat pears from the backyard tree. We play with dolls and wagons, tricycles and cap guns until we tire of each other.

Daddy comes home from the office to eat dinner. He walks in with a stack of mail and The Birmingham Post Herald under his arm. He picks me up, in his teasing way and I smell his fresh white shirt. My daddy holds me tight, pokes at my ribs and tickles me until I laugh so hard I can't breathe.

The afternoon grows weary and I sit on the porch with my books. On this day, Mama reads aloud to me.

After supper, all of the neighbors gather under the tree with the branches and leaves that practically spread from my grandmother's house to mine. They sit in Adirondack chairs, share conversation and laugh. Their voices become muffled with the rising sounds of Katydids.

I run with the other children and catch lightning bugs, put them in a jar and let them go to light up the night once again.

The neighbors slowly rise from chairs and begin walking across squeaky grass toward their homes. I say, "goodnight" to my friends and don't dread the bath that awaits me. Bubbles and soothing water slacken my resistance to crawling into bed.

I look out my bedroom window and watch lights being turned out in houses that line our street.

It would be a simple day that I would choose to visit.

No big deal.

Just the loneliness that lingers with me now.

LIFE AND ART

There I stood. On the corner of University Boulevard and Sorority row. They drove off. Three hours back to the home that would probably never really be home to me again. They couldn't stay and lead me around by the hand.

Mama and Daddy had attended The University of Alabama. It was sort of unspoken that I would go. Not only would I go, but I would be in a sorority where "I would grow culturally and socially."

When my ACT test scores arrived at the high school, the sum total was low. If it hadn't been for my English grade alone, I wouldn't have been a college student anywhere, and I wouldn't be telling this story. Who would have thought that English grammar would be the deciding factor in my acceptance to a school where all I wanted to do was draw.

I was almost eighteen years old. I had never driven a car except to the store in my small hometown. I had never had a real date. I did not know how to read a map. Panic set in and tears spilled out from behind my hard, blue-tinted contact lenses. I crossed the street and headed toward the quadrangle.

The large plot of land in the center of the University was dotted with old, giant trees and surrounded by massive buildings. I didn't know one direction from another, so I cried and walked and cried. I had never been in such a huge place alone in all of my life. I hated it all and I would show Mama! I'd drop her sacred sorority the first day.

The ritual of sorority Rush was exhausting and brutal. Beautifully quaffed, impeccably coordinated girls with summer tans and white toothy smiles greeted us at the doors of Southern mansions. We were escorted into carpeted rooms where our Bass Weejun loafers sunk into thick pile. Crystal cups filled with punch and plates of delicate cookies were gracefully handed to us.

We were treated as if we were the most gorgeous, important young ladies on the planet. Then, in the blink of any eye, we'd be dropped like hot potatoes. Each morning we gathered like lemmings to open our envelopes. Hundreds of girls in Foster Auditorium sat on metal folding chairs in that hot, multi-purpose gymnasium.

We were apprehensive as we tore into envelopes which held our fate on a cream-colored card. We discovered who was pushed off of which "lovely southern manor cliff," and who would be invited to the next round of parties.

Girls either stood up and squealed with excitement or sat and sobbed in their chairs. Emotions echoed off of bleachers and basketball goals. I did as I planned. I dropped Mama's, Pi Beta Phi, after the first day. Little did I know that Tri Delta, Alpha Gam and many more would drop me immediately or keep me dangling until he last day.

No one wanted me and I was up sludge creek without a paddle. I would be an embarrassment to Mama and all of her friends. I'd join the ranks of the "independents," heaven forbid! Independents wore thick glasses and had zits. They studied all of the time and didn't have roommates. They wore tacky clothes, had dirty hair and bad breath. That's what my friend, Marsha told me, anyway.

Pi Beta Phi learned of my predicament and conferred. Their records showed that my name had not been delegated to the "pig box" on "Ice Water Tea Day." I was a "legacy" because My mama was one of the tried and true, wine and silver blue Pi Beta Phis. My daddy was respected in our community and held an important position in his company. They didn't know that Daddy WAS the company in a hole in the wall office, and that we were "comfortable" but not rich.

Although I had dropped the sorority because I was mad at Mama, they took me into their fold anyway. I bawled like a baby and felt guilty. When the members all hugged me and said how happy they were to have me, I felt like the scum of the earth.

Behind those sweet southern sorority girl smiles, were some party animals. I learned to cuss and drink shots of Tequila. I tried smoking but threw up after a few drags. Those girls looked so beautiful and sophisticated holding their cigarettes. They sat with their legs crossed and flicked ashes into silver "Pi Beta Phi" ashtrays. Now, I'm thankful I couldn't pull off smoking.

Being in that house on sorority row WAS a cultural and social experience. The kind I needed to get me out of my shell. And if the truth be known, I imagine it wasn't all that different from when my mama was there thirty-five years before.

It was unacceptable to stay in on Friday and Saturday nights, so the Phi Phis made sure their girls had dates every weekend. No one even had to ask me out. I just went with whoever they fixed me up with. Very few fraternity men had cars in the sixties. Our dates would pick us up at the door and we'd walk to fraternity parties or concerts. Sometimes, we would make the long walk into downtown Tuscaloosa to see a movie.

One Saturday night, the boy I was paired up with, told me that we'd be double dating in a car. The word, "car" conjured up feelings of having no control. Of speeding through the night into unknown territory. strange, male arms clutching me and a sweaty face trying to invade my lips. I was sick at the thought. We made it to the event at a campus auditorium but I was consumed by where we might go later in the evening.

After what I considered to be a reasonable amount of time, I excused myself to go to the ladies room. I opened a heavy door to the starlit, cool night and took off running like a bat out of hell. I ran for blocks, imagining that the boy was behind me. I I sucked air of freedom into my lungs, and did not stop until I reached the safety of my dorm room.

In the nineteen sixties, girls went to college to find a husband. We were there for that reason first, social and cultural development second, and somewhat of an education, third. If a girl didn't graduate from college, that was fine. Just so she had a husband or at least a fiancé. A boy was expected to graduate so that he could support his wife and future children.

I wasn't really interested in finding a husband. But I was terrified of being an old maid. So, I latched onto the first boy who gave me "the time of day." I guess we thought we were in love, but we were so terribly young. We married right after college, had two sons and hung on for twenty years.

Things were bound to change for young women. And change wasn't too far down the road in the mid-sixties.

Arrowboard was formed to keep a handle on the morality of the girls. The board was made up of officers in our sorority establishment. The officers were set apart as shining examples of what the upstanding southern young lady should be. Sorority girls did imbibe on occasion but we certainly knew the importance of "appearances". If we slipped and forgot about "appearances," we were called before Arrowboard to be reprimanded.

I kissed my boyfriend too long at the front door and was reported by one of my "dear sisters" in Pi Beta Phi. I had committed the crime of, PDA (public display of affection) and knew I'd have to take my sentence like a lady. I entered the "courtroom," stood before a table surrounded by stern faced authority figures who were only a year or two older than I, and received my sentence.

Two weekends confined to the sorority house. No parties. No boyfriend. I had observed those solemn judges at times: Lipstick all over their faces, matted hair and hickies too obvious to be hidden by Cover Girl's Erase or turtle neck sweaters. It was all so ludicrous. I had to laugh inside.

The innocent kid from the small town learned her way around that big campus. I felt independence for the first time in my life and really liked the taste of it. Of course, we had curfews and were required to be in our dorms by nine o'clock on week-nights. On the weekends we were allowed to stay out until 11:30.

I could have danced non-stop at fraternity parties. Thumping sounds of Black soul music rocked the floors where rugs had been rolled up. Lionel Ritchie and other future "names" played and sang in those sweat filled rooms. Their music would stay with me forever, and the rhythm would never let my feet be still.

The University of Alabama Art Department was housed in Woods Hall, a rectangle of buildings facing a courtyard. Popular Ivy League fashions, plaids, khaki and penny loafers, clashed with an atmosphere that began with the very buildings themselves.

Woods Hall buildings had been constructed in the eighteen hundreds for use as a military school and barracks. The ancient rickety buildings with their huge rooms made perfect settings for large canvases, thick with paint. The paintings seemed to continue onto the floors and walls, out the doors and onto the jeans and torn blue work shirts of "serious art students."

Technically, women were not allowed to wear jeans or slacks on campus during the school week. We women art students got around the strict rule by wearing our tan, monogrammed London Fog raincoats over grubby clothes. We worried about being expelled if the dean of women ever caught us. We'd race across the quadrangle with our heads down, as if such a posture might make us invisible.

Professors gave their commentaries and criticisms with screaming voices and dramatic displays of artistic authority. One particular teacher tore his students' work to shreds and stomped on the ragged pieces of paper, when random patterns offended him. This was abstract expressionism. It made no sense and was not what I came for. But it was the nineteen sixties.

At the beginning of my junior year, I climbed the stairs of one of the Woods Hall buildings. I noticed a faint pleasant aroma, drifting down to meet me. It was not the usual pungent turpentine, linseed oil and paint. This smell was different, and the room at the top of the stairs was different. Drafting tables were neatly lined up. The floors were shiny with no signs of spilled paint. Windows stood side by side all around the room and I had never seen so much light in any of my classes before.

Students were assuming their positions at the tables and opening metal tool boxes, which were staples and badges of art majors. From a small studio in the back of the room, emerged a very pleasant looking man with a pipe in his hand. That was the smell! The pipe.

Mr. Brough stood in direct opposition to the other professors. He was slightly round and wore a sweater vest with a clean shirt underneath. His rolled-up sleeves gave him a casual, approachable appearance. The crease in his slacks went down to meet nice brown shoes. He spoke in a mild pleasant tone and welcomed us to the school of commercial art.

We would soon discover that in addition to his knowledge of graphic arts, Mr. Brough was an extremely talented watercolorist. His subject matter was taken from the world around us. Nature, buildings, people. Nonobjective painting had it's place and purpose in art. But I wanted instruction. I wanted to be the best I could be when it came to drawing. Mr. Brough was my ticket to learning and I'd better absorb everything he had to offer.

I often stood outside on the third floor of one particular Woods Hall building. I'd be wearing my very stylish, slightly artsy coat, the color of yellow ochre paint. I'd look out onto the quadrangle and feel the wind blowing my shiny strawberry blonde hair.

I was aware that I made a pretty picture, and was proud of the fact that none of the old high school boys back home recognized me anymore. But there was a strong stirring inside my heart. I knew that I was right there in the moment, and that when I left college, life would never imitate that world. I wanted to keep the picture intact and hang onto a time that would pass way too quickly. I would miss it all.

My daddy didn't really think I would graduate from college, so he promised to buy me a brand new car if I did. He referred to a graduation certificate as a "sheepskin." I guess that's what they called it when he was in school. He told me that if I got that "sheepskin," I'd get a car.

I don't know exactly how I managed to do it. I think it was my passion for art. I didn't have to try so hard to make good grades in my major. The first two years were rough because of required subjects. Psychology nearly killed me, but I passed with a, D. Those required subjects were like a roller coaster ride. Some pulled me up and others made me spiral down. I liked English and language classes. Somehow it all worked out, and the shiny, new yellow 1967 Chevrolet Impala was waiting for me at the end of the line.

Passing by Bear Bryant at the student union building and seeing Joe Namath waiting for his date at the dorm were common occurrences. But, Mr. Brough was my real hero. He created a haven. Order out of chaos in the crazy sixties.

Sometimes when fall is in the air, I can smell musty books, bourbon, Linseed oil and Mr. Brough's pipe all mingled together. I stand in my home art studio and look at implements saved from school. I use them as art in themselves. Items for displaying in my cabinet. There is a picture of Mr. Brough, my old drafting set, brushes that I kept, and a framed assignment with a grade of B+ in the corner.

My career as a painter has been long and rewarding. I wouldn't go back to being a college girl, but I surely do get twinges of nostalgia, like when wood smoke brings memories of camp. And lightning bugs in summer make me wish, for a moment, that I was a child again.

FOOD FOR THE BIRDS

It was late afternoon. No glorious sunset to watch from our folding chairs. The sky, sea and damp sand glistened, and were coated with shades of gray and brown.

The girl caught sight of me as I furiously snapped pictures of her. She wore faded, cropped overalls that blended with the colors of the day. Her small hands threw pieces of bread upward, to be gratefully caught by flapping, squealing seagulls. The birds surrounded her and sounded as if they could have lifted her small body to the sky.

She ran excitedly toward me and asked, "Are you a photographer?" "No," I replied. "I'm a painter. I might paint your picture with the birds. Would you like that?" "Yeah!" was her childish response.

"My cousin was an artist," she offered. "Oh, really? Does he still paint?" "He died. We're having the 'awakening' tonight. Nobody wants to look at the paintings. It makes them sad. They're all put away. He was eighteen."

"Oh, I'm so sorry to hear that." "That's ok," she called out as she ran hastily back to her recreation. The child's hair blew into and out of her face as she threw bread to the sky.

When dark came, we folded our chairs and headed for our cabin on the beach.

I turned and took one last look at the girl. Her overalls were wet at the bottom, and formed a blurry pattern of deep indigo. Her family called her name, she ran toward them, and the seagulls fluttered off in search of food from another source.

I painted the picture, and as I worked wet into dry, rough watercolor paper, I wondered. What could have happened to a young artist? Was he lonely, depressed? Did he suffer from the malady known to creative people? An illness, an accident?

I gaze upon the finished piece, tastefully matted and framed, and step back to look at the recreated scene.

"Artistic license" allows for luxurious rich pigment. Sunset's golden hues touch the girl's clothing and hair. The water is Prussian Blue, Winsor Green and Purple Madder.

Seagulls are splashed with the sun's setting rays. Color bounces everywhere. And the gray day of death is gone.

ELEANOR WILLOUGHBY

Some of it was told to me and some came from living and observing. From the eyes and mind of a three year old child until fifty years later when my grandmother died at age ninety eight.

Eleanor Willoughby Rice was new in town and eighteen years old when she spotted Otto. Otto Brice had a motorcycle, worked at his daddy's general store and was a dashing eligible young man. "Willie" assumed she didn't stand a chance. She underestimated her large crystal blue eyes and natural ability to sachet around the bustling town of Oneonta, Alabama during the early 1900s.

Otto did notice Willie. He was very interested, and scribbled a question on a piece of paper from the store. He told one of the young workers to take the note, run down the street and give it to the pretty girl in the blue dress.

Flirtatious meetings began and it didn't take long for Otto to propose marriage. But Willie's answer was a disappointing, "no." She had accepted a teaching job in the countryside and planned to move there. Otto must have been confident in his ability to woo his love because he had already arranged for Byrd School to hire another teacher. Willie's answer became an emphatic, "yes!"

Willie worried about her father who didn't have much money. She grew up in a family of nine sisters and a brother. So, instead of asking for a wedding, she and one of her girlfriends began to scheme. Willie sneaked off, rode the train to Birmingham and bought her trousseau.

Willie and Otto eloped. Although Willie's intentions were good, I don't think her papa was pleased with his youngest daughter's unconventional behavior. This was not the beginning or the end of unconventionality in Willie's nature.

Otto Brice had a pet name for my grandmother. Her maiden name was, Rice, so he forever referred to her as "Ricie." The name stuck and years later she was called, "Ricie" by my cousin, Karen and me. We were her only grandchildren.

From all accounts, my grandfather had a quick wit and magnetic personality. I listened to stories about his sense of humor and antics. He was adored by his daughter and the feeling was mutual. He was somewhat stern with my father, a red-headed freckled-faced fireball with a history of endless plots and concocted stories. A child of dangerous inventions and electric curiosity.

On father's day, in the early 1940s, Otto died suddenly, without warning. The family was still young. The shock and loss from this unexpected tragedy, linger in my daddy's heart over fifty years later.

Eleanor Willoughby was strong. She was a young widow, but she went on with her life. She involved herself in town and church organizations, garden and study clubs. Her interests and contributions continued throughout her life. She gave an impeccable speech, without notes, to the Historical Society, two weeks before she died.

Ricie lived in a huge rambling house. It was the home Otto had built for his wife and children. When I was three years old, we moved next door to my grandmother. Ricie owned the little bungalow house, so Daddy paid the rent while we lived there for seven years. I loved being within running distance of Ricie. Her house had an upstairs with rooms everywhere. She had a piano to bang on and a wrap-around porch with gliders, swings and rocking chairs.

Ricie wasn't the "grandmotherly" type. She wasn't physically affectionate, but that was ok with me. I never liked being smothered and kissed by older people anyway. She didn't like to cook, but did it out of necessity. And there was always delicious sweet ice tea to drink at her kitchen table. She wasn't too keen on babysitting me because her life was filled with books, women friends, club meetings and games of Canasta. She drove her Packard wherever she liked.

Occasionally, I did spend the night with Ricie. I think she liked me better as I got older. Even with all of the bedrooms in her house, I chose to sleep in the bed beside her. I was leery of the upstairs in the dark. I found her nighttime ritual interesting. It never varied. She would emerge from the bathroom slathering Pond's Cold Cream on her face. A hairnet pressed down on her tightly curled permanent wave. The bedside light was on, giving me full view of her ceremonious acts. She stood beside the bed, raised her arms up as high as they would go, then bent down to touch her toes. She did this exercise repeatedly, counting to fifty or a hundred.

Then, she snapped out the light. But from the street lights I could see her on her knees, hands folded, head bowed. These prayers lasted about five minutes. She stood up, slid in beside me and said, "Goodnight, Janet." "Night," I replied.

Mornings were light and airy. The big old house smelled of soap, flowers and fresh air. Ricie took her bath early and dressed in stockings, a crisp flattering dress and "old lady" black or white shoes depending upon the season. She loved clothes and knew beyond a shadow of a doubt that, at her mature age, she was still attractive. Her blue eyes never faded.

In the summers, Ricie's porch overflowed with her knack for growing things. Ferns cascaded over the banisters and invited passers-by to ascend the concrete steps for a visit. If neighbors were still rocking and talking at noon, my grandmother would jump up from her chair and announce, "It's time to eat." She wasn't offering a place at her table, she was stating her schedule.

At noon, she ate her main meal, cleaned up the dishes and then napped for thirty minutes. She lay on top of her bed, shoes, dress, stockings and all. She walked daily and ate supper at 5:00 on the dot.

When my grandmother was in her eighties, she decided to take a job. There was an opening at the county historical museum and she was perfect for the position. She was a wealth of information for visitors and was asked to write her memories of growing up in Blount county.

Ricie had always been interested in other people. She didn't talk about herself very much. She would sit in her rocking chair on the porch across from whoever stopped by. She asked people questions about their families and activities. I grew to admire that quality in my grandmother.

After she wrote for the Historical Society newsletter, I wanted to know more. I wanted to hear anything she would tell me about her experiences.

And so she did. Ricie told me about her eccentric mother who had eleven children. My great-grandmother, Kate Willoughby Rice, was afraid to ride in a horse-drawn carriage over the covered bridges in Blount County. She worried about herself, over and above her children and husband. So, when the family approached a bridge, Kate got out and waited for the carriage make it's way to the other side. Then she lightly walked across the bridge to safety.

Kate spent her days reading. She left her youngest children in the care of the oldest ones. When the sun sank low and created an orange glow on her book, she stood up, patted her hair and smoothed out her apron. She knew that her husband would soon begin his trek home from working in the fields. Kate hustled her girls to help prepare a meal and make the house appear orderly. But all Kate ever really wanted to do was read.

When my grandmother was a child, she ran down the dirt road that led from Ricetown to Blount Springs. She wanted to get away from her country home. She and her sisters ran down that road with their braids flying. They were impatiently leaving behind one life for another, much more glamorous one.

The girls were hot from running, and burning with anticipation for what was to come. Their rosy cheeks glowed as the dust settled around their feet and they looked up at the glorious structure standing before them.

The hotel in Blount Springs, Alabama was massive and beautiful. The air was pure, the entertainment and relaxation, sublime. The train blew it's whistle, screeched to a stop, and created such a display of elegance. A band played as beautifully dressed women and handsome men stepped off of the train. Their leather luggage was shiny and expensive looking. Willie could just imagine trunks piled with gorgeous dresses and jewelry.

Rushing and bubbling springs surrounding the hotel, were thought to be healing. Hotel guests drank the putrid tasting sulfur water, believing that they would be cured of whatever ailed them. Willie and her sisters thought it amusing that people would drink a liquid which smelled and tasted so awful. There was even a factory that bottled the water, so rich people could take it home with them in blue bottles.

Everything about Blount Springs made Willie tingle with excitement. In addition to glamour and lavish lifestyles , the area held a secret air of mystery which filled children's minds with contrived stories and imagined fear.

In a small cabin in the mountains, lived a "witch." At least, that's what the children surmised. They had never seen her, but had heard about the woman who lived there. They listened to adults talk about her reclusiveness and antisocial behavior. The fantasies grew and fear became surmountable.

Willie, Maude and Annie found it difficult to walk the wooded path without making sounds. Leaves crunched and twigs popped, but their pounding hearts were all they heard.

"Let's go back" whispered Annie. "No! we've come this far," commanded Maude. The cabin came into view and the three girls stopped dead in their tracks. But they had to know. They just had to see for themselves. They moved forward, raced toward a side window of the small house and stooped down. Slowly, the three of them rose until their eyes and noses met the window sill.

They could see a small woman, reclining on her bed. She was reading. She turned toward the window, saw the three girls looking at her, and said, "Well, hello there. Won't you come in?"

Willie could not believe her ears. They walked around to the porch, up a few steps and into a cozy room lined with books. Mary Gordon Duffee had plants of every kind spread out on tables. Colorful flowers were placed in glass jars. She had pages and pages of hand-written paper. A fire crackled in the fireplace and the whole place smelled delicious.

The famous writer offered the girls cookies and apples. She showed them books which said, "By, Mary Gordon Duffee" on the covers. She told them that she wrote about nature and beautiful flowers that grew wild in the Alabama woods. The charming lady was indeed, not a witch. She waved good-bye to the girls and told them to stop by again.

Willie continued her fasination with the Blount Springs Hotel. As she skipped down the road from Ricetown, she thought about how her father, Jake was opposed to dancing. But not Willie. Dancing was a freedom in her spirit and the lovely ballroom called her to peep through the windows.

Music poured out of the building, around the mountains and through the bubbling springs. Willie couldn't wait to grow up. She wanted to learn about plants like Miss Duffee and dance 'til her heart's content.

DRIVING AUNT SALLY

Aunt Sally was rich. She owned six movie theaters in Birmingham, Alabama. That's where I lived with Mama, Daddy and my much older sister, Vivian. Our small apartment was right down the street from Aunt Sally's mansion.

My daddy was not rich. He managed one of Aunt Sally's picture shows, but owning a theater and working for one are two different things entirely. But, I'm not complaining, because we had it pretty good. Aunt Sally was a generous rich lady and she treated our family well.

Aunt Sally had been married to Mama's brother, Marvin. Uncle Marvin died and left Aunt Sally a widow with two girls. The two girls, Sarah and Alice were close to my age and we spent a lot of time together.

I loved going over to their big house and spending the night. I liked those long halls and big rooms, but most of all I liked being with my cousins and away from my bossy sister. They had cooks and maids and a private chauffer.

Everyday, the chauffer would pull that big black Cadillac up in front of Aunt Sally's long porch and take my aunt downtown to check on her picture shows. The Empire, The Melba, The Lyric, The Strand, The Royal and The Capitol.

Aunt Sally had a dry, southern sense of humor. She had a deep voice and punctuated her conversation with "hells" and "damns." She was quite a character, and her daughter, Sarah was a lot like her. Alice was quieter, and I was the quietest of all. My shyness hindered my entire youth and I wish I could go back and burst out of that inhibiting shell. But I can't and that's that.

I didn't think much of myself, but I did know that I was fairly pretty. I guess that's the only thing I had to hang on to. The boys looked at me, but I was too afraid to flirt with them. I wasn't shy around Aunt Sally, Sarah and Alice. I felt comfortable and free.

Speaking of free, our families got to see all the free movies we wanted, and as many times as we wanted to see them. I saw King Kong twenty-seven times and never got tired of it.

I got Sarah and Alice's hand-me-down clothes, which were just like new, and my mama could sew like a professional. With Mama's seamstress abilities and my cousins' barely worn dresses, I was pretty well set in the nineteen thirties. Aunt Sally bought me nice jewelry and took me on trips, just like I was one of her daughters. One of those trips was an experience I'll never forget.

The sheets and pillowcases felt and smelled rich at Aunt Sally's house. I reclined and propped on a pile of luxurious pillows on Alice's bed. Sarah, Alice and I were sitting there together and talking nonstop. Alice and I were fifteen and Sarah was sixteen. Aunt Sally was going to chaperone the three of us on a trip to Pensacola, Florida and we could hardly wait. School was out, the weather was warm and our bags were packed.

We'd be staying in a fancy hotel and we'd get to eat in fine restaurants. I was glad my sister was seven years older than I. She was too old to be interested in going anywhere with us.

Vivian attended college, but still lived at home. Soon she would be graduating and I was hoping she'd find a husband and move out. She thought she was my mama, so I had to put up with two mamas. No wonder Daddy went off with Uncle Grover, Uncle Edwin and a bunch of men to that cabin down in Montgomery. Too many women around.

Sarah could drive, and she loved it! The chauffer stayed home. Aunt Sally sat up front by Sarah. Alice and I sat in the back seat. We headed south and drove through towns with beautiful homes and quiet streets. The longer the moss hung down on the trees, the more drawn-out people's accents became. When we stopped for gas and Cokes, slow southern drawls welcomed us and the easy-going pace intrigued us. We were city girls, used to big buildings, traffic and noise. What a nice change!

We were about two hours away from our destination when Alice said she smelled something funny. We all sniffed, and agreed that something was burning. We decided it was probably coming from the area we were passing through. Sarah's lead foot never let up. Then we saw the smoke seeping out from under the hood. Sarah kept on flying down the road.

Aunt Sally had already told Sarah to slow down. "Say-rah, you bettah damn way-ell stop this cah right na-ow cauz we gonna git th hell outta here!" Aunt Sally's words carried some weight that time. Sarah came to a screeching halt, and by that time, the smoke had turned into flames.

We were absolutely NOT going to lose the clothes and cosmetics we had so thoughtfully packed, so Sarah opened the trunk and we pulled out every suitcase just in time for all of us to run across the road.

We watched as black paint bubbled and melted off of the once shiny Cadillac. The car started jerking and bumping like crazy. It rattled itself off of the road, rolled over and blew up. A huge cloud of orange fire and blue smoke created a major attraction in slow-moving south Alabama.

The four of us stood beside a sparse palm tree and thanked the Lord we were out of that car. Aunt Sally shielded her eyes with her hand, but her fine hat was still on her head. She wore a pale blue dress, stockings and white lace-up shoes. We stood close together, holding our suitcases, and not knowing exactly what to do next.

After a while, Aunt Sally broke the silence. "I've got evah kind uv insurance in th world except car insurance." She broke out laughing. We looked at her and then we started laughing. We got hysterical and tears were rolling down our faces. Aunt Sally said, "I'll jus buy uh-nutha one."

Back in those days, people stopped to help, and everyone trusted most people. One of the families who stopped to watch the commotion, invited us to go to their house. We gratefully packed our baggage and ourselves into their car and headed to the home of generous strangers.

We freshened ourselves up in their bathroom, and congregated on their porch. In typical southern hospitality style, our hosts served us sandwiches and cold drinks. We relaxed and conversed, and, naturally found out that they knew some of the same people we knew. By the end of the visit, we were practically related.

Aunt Sally called a taxi, and the taxi took us to Pensacola. Aunt Sally said we were not going to spoil our good time just because the car blew up. A whole week to play in the ocean, walk on the beach, eat snacks and stay up late!

Sarah was the most glamorous of the three of us. She was tall, thin, blonde and tan. Alice was beautiful with black hair, flawless skin and green eyes. I was tall for fifteen, but wouldn't stand up straight and show off my height. I was skinny and gangly, pale and blonde. But I was pretty enough, and we all attracted attention.

I am eighty-three now. How on earth did I get to be so old?! I am sitting here looking at a black and white picture from that trip. I'm wearing a summery, stripped cotton dress with a sailor collar. My waist is the size of a pencil! Standing beside me is a boy. I'll never know who he was. For all I know, he's living right here in Essex Place. One of those babbling old men who bores everyone to death telling about their past accomplishments.

Oh, my, where did the time go? I'm looking at that picture and tears are rolling down my face. I am laughing myself silly. What a hell of a good time we all had!

AMANDA'S CHILD

Amanda lived in a world of her own. She'd sit at the kitchen table and slowly turn her head toward the window. Outside, her sister, Jennifer, my two boys and a whole neighborhood of children rode bicycles, skateboards and played as if they were trying to outrun the short days of fall.

Amanda liked to be around me but the feeling was not always mutual. She followed me from one room to another. At times, my irritation would be thrown headlong into a sudden invitation to join her world.

Some color or design in a throw pillow compared to an element of nature. A painting or decorative corner brought endless questions. This eight year old child noticed beauty and creativity. She longed to be creative. It was obvious to me that she already was.

Amanda and Jennifer had clear green eyes set against porcelain faces. Thick black hair framed their beautiful little features. They were direct opposites from my sons, Brice and Joe, who were strawberry-blonde and freckled.

Joe and Jennifer were in kindergarten together and had a year long romance. They kissed under the stairs of the condominium clubhouse and Joe gave Jennifer a necklace to seal their love. Brice and Amanda tolerated each other.

The girls' mother, Ellen was my best friend. I kept her daughters after school until she returned home from working as a nurse. Ellen wore a stiff white hat, knee length dress and white stockings. As soon as she got home from work, she'd come over to my apartment so we could spend time together.

Ellen was a surgery nurse at a nearby hospital. She had no qualms about recounting details of surgical procedures. She could talk about the most disgusting things while downing a whole jar of peanuts followed by pickled okra.

Ellen and I were married to bar-hopping womanizers who came home at will. We became a family out of necessity and loneliness. In spite of everything, our children seemed happy and unaffected by our distress.

The condo complex had a pool and wide-spread grounds for kids to play and have adventures. At the edge of the woods, they built a rambling, tree house, hide-out, with rooms and ladders and old carpet. The construction of that retreat never ended. It gave the children pleasure and something to look forward to on weekends and after school.

So many future "Generation X-ers" were being raised by single parents. They were part of mixtures so confusing, they didn't know who their step, half, or whole brothers and sisters were. Now, the label is "blended family."

Some of the children were given freedom to "be" while their hippie parents gathered in groups, listened to music, drank, cried and contemplated the meaning of life. I joined a few of those soirees just observe. Although my husband loved the bar scene, he also had a "sensitive side." He wore beads and developed "deep" relationships with men and women. I thought it was all a crock. The whole ridiculous scene made me sick.

Ellen joined this nineteen seventies craziness occasionally, mostly out of curiosity. But, Ellen knew the truth that the rest of us were blind to. Ellen's spirit was free in a completely different way from the "navel gazers." It would be years before I knew anything about that.

As our children grew, Ellen and I grew in our friendship. We confided in each other and shared our innermost thoughts and dreams. We went to movies and out to dinner. We were lonely and knew that our marriages couldn't possibly last forever.

Our children grew tired of each other. They had become like siblings. The boys complained when I kept the girls and they complained when they were left in the care of Ellen.

Amanda was beginning to have trouble in school. She couldn't concentrate and her grades were low. Jennifer was bouncy and smart which made the comparative situation worse. Amanda was affected by her father's behavior.

Without a father's presence and without motivation to do better in school, Amanda slipped into a crowd of friends who liked her and led her toward negative choices.

Ellen tried to keep the family going. She went back to school to get another nursing degree and worked at the same time. When she realized the severity of Amanda's situation, she felt helpless.

For many years, Ellen did not know where her wayward child was. There were nights of searching, calling friends and the police. All of this took a toll on Ellen. Amanda finally grew up and joined the military.

Ellen let go, gave up and turned her over to God. They didn't communicate and it seemed better that way.

Jennifer was in college and planning a teaching career. Brice and Joe were doing well at their universities. Ellen and I found our "Prince Charmings" and remarried. My husband, Eddie, and I were building a house, and my life was better than it had ever been. But, that "mother thing" never goes away. It can rip you to pieces. Once a child exits the womb, I do believe that a mother's heart acquires a weight that is never lifted.

The three hour distance between Ellen's town and mine didn't change our friendship. We were "sisters" and always would be. Our relationship grew stronger with each phone call, visit, agreement and disagreement.

Ellen traveled from her town, to ours. We had planned to spend a few days together to celebrate our birthdays, which were two days apart. She drove up to the tiny, rental house my husband and I occupied during our building process. The house was packed to the hilt with boxes and furniture.

For a touch of whimsy, I had placed an outdoor table set with opened umbrella in the kitchen. The three of us sat under that umbrella, but there was no air of celebration. Ellen looked worse than I had ever seen her. Helping each other through times of trouble had always been a part of our relationship. But for Ellen, this was bad.

Eddie grew up with sisters, girl cousins and many female friends, so he was perfectly comfortable sitting quietly with us. He was sympathetic to women's ups, downs and crying spells. Ellen wasn't crying, she was pale and shaky.

After a couple of glasses of wine, Ellen announced that Amanda was pregnant. I asked when the baby was due. "She may have already had it," was her response. "The father is Black." We learned that Amanda was married to the man, so I didn't understand the problem. The problem, it seems was not the man's heritage, but that his very being was a culmination of the bad choices Amanda had been making for years. Amanda never thought she deserved anything good.

Three years later, Amanda had produced two more children. She was still in the military. Her husband had been kicked out. He wrecked cars, went to jail, neglected the children and abused Amanda. Amanda stayed.

I had always been a second mother to Amanda. She called me in 1993 with the news that the military was sending her to Haiti. Her husband's parents agreed to keep the two youngest children but she had no place to leave her firstborn, Jessie.

Amanda was "still following me from room to room." "Mom can't do it" Amanda told me. I understood. Ellen worked at a hospital and I worked at my home art studio.

"Of course we'll take her," Eddie said without hesitation. I thought Amanda was going to break down from relief and gratitude.

Eddie and I drove three hours to pick up Jessie. We arrived, parked the car and looked at each other with fear and excitement. It would be our first time to meet Amanda's oldest child. She was beautiful! She had Amanda's perfect features and a tan to die for. But, I was going to have to do something about that hair.

Jessie knew she was coming to live with us. She had no concept of time and didn't care. She bounced into the van and made herself at home. We purchased the van a year before and it just happened to have pull-out regulation child seats. Things work out the way they are supposed to.

Years ago, Ellen had shared her faith in God with me. The freedom she always carried with her. If Eddie and I had never understood the grace she spoke of, we wouldn't have taken Jessie. We were selfish and enjoyed our time alone together. But that was a responsibility we needed to accept.

That first morning, Jessie slept late. She must have been exhausted. She came downstairs wearing Eddie's T-shirt. Her bristly hair was standing straight up at least six inches from her scalp. I fixed eggs, bacon, pancakes and cereal. She ate every bit, drank orange juice, milk and wanted more. I had never seen a three year old eat like that. She would soon be four, on October 20. Exactly one week after my birthday. I guess she was growing.

A major shopping trip to Wal-Mart was in order. Jessie had the clothes she wore home with us and that was it. This was going to be fun. I could feel myself going overboard even before we left. Shoes, dresses, jeans, shirts! Our trip also included the mall where Jessie rode the carousal, ate ice cream and picked out more stuff. Of course we needed toys! How could a child learn, be creative, grasp concepts without toys?!

The hair had to go. I did not raise girls and I knew I couldn't deal with the everyday maintenance of that texture. I got the scissors out, took one big whack and Jessie screamed bloody murder. She wanted long hair like Barbie but I knew she'd get over it. Her short, soft brown curls were shiny and the gel made them even better. There was still plenty left to put a bow in. She liked it.

As the days and weeks passed, Eddie and I became aware that Jessie was far behind her peers in many ways. Her speech was limited, she did not know colors, numbers or letters. I suppose Sesame Street hadn't been available to her. And no one had taken the time to read those repetitive stories every child needs. All of that changed. I don't know what Eddie and I thought when we accepted the position of Jessie's caretakers. I do know that it was much harder, more stressful, fun, miserable and rewarding than we ever imagined.

I've always enjoyed hanging around women who are younger than I am. Women my age seem, well...old. Our church was full of young couples with kids, so I learned the ropes of their routines. Some of the ropes were not appealing to me. Certain fast-food restaurants made me gag and that reflex was intensified by watching the kids eat. Weekly early morning skate time for youngsters became part of my new life.

If Jessie didn't have someone to play with, she wanted me to play with her. I don't like to play. But I did enjoy setting up a corner of my art studio for her so she could experiment with painting. I read to her constantly, she learned to name the magnetic letters on the refrigerator, and colors became part of everyday life. Eddie and I took her to the beach for a week, we took her to Seaworld, parades and festivals. Any and everything that would stimulate that little mind.

After four months, we were physically and emotionally spent. Eddie and I loved this child immensely.

We felt like she belonged to us. We didn't want to give her up but I had lost fifteen pounds and people were starting to ask me if I had a serious illness. We had no idea how long Amanda would be in Haiti. We had to have a break.

Jessie's father's parents were willing to take her. They were nice people. But something was odd. Jessie didn't look anything like them. She didn't look anything like her younger brother and sister. Her brother and sister looked like each other, but Jessie looked like Amanda and someone we would probably never know. Ellen had already figured it out.

Although I had no idea who Jessie's real father was or what he was like, I was relieved to know that she was not biologically related to the man she called, "Daddy."

Eddie and I were alone again. Grateful and sad. We missed the little child we had fallen in love with. But, we went to the beach, slept late, ate and talked without being interrupted. I became fat and happy again and painted in my studio.

After about eight months, Amanda called again for help. It was the middle of the night. She was beaten down and battered. We took Jessie again and again.

Thankfully, Jessie has continued to be a part of our lives. After years of destructive choices, Amanda seems to be doing better. She divorced her abusive husband, has a stable job and cares for her three children.

Jessie is twelve years old. She is beautiful, bright and can braid her own long hair. She is smart and full of scientific facts that I know nothing about. We have changed places. She helps me when I get fowled up on the computer. Eddie and I spoil her rotten when she comes to stay with us in the summers.

Ellen is taking an active role in the lives of her grandchildren. Jessie's teenage years are right around the corner. A frightening thought for all of us who are participating in raising her.

I pray that Jessie's voice and footsteps will fill this old country house for years to come and that the positive parent figures in her life will give her hope and strength. I pray that she will choose wisely. I hope Amanda will know the good and the worth in herself. That she will look into the eyes of her children and see what God has entrusted to her care.

TIME CHANGE

Something had gone wrong in Marie's young life that day in 1952. The huge old house was teeming with people. Cousins, aunts, uncles, grandparents and friends. I turned a corner and saw the eight-year old child standing in a dark hallway that was void of life. A shadow of movement stirred one of the rooms. Something fleeting, that I couldn't make out. A swift breeze caused the stiff curtains to snap and relax as if no air had stirred at all. Sharp streaks of sunlight revealed things, out of place. A sense of confusion and disorder, was as thick as the heat in the hallway.

She looked up at me, as if to beg for help. Fear and shame held my gaze. "Tell me what happened, Marie." The words would not come, and my heart ached for the child. I knew, at that moment, I was going to walk out of the house and take Marie with me.

Marie had a chopped off bob of a haircut. She had luminous skin dotted with freckles, and crisp blue eyes. But I could see her scars. I could see the hurt in her past, and the hurt that was to come.

I grabbed Marie's hand and rushed down the back stairs. I clutched my purse and keys, and opened the heavy back door. I could hear her leather-soled Mary Janes tap on the brick walkway as we hurriedly approached the car. The rhythm of our steps sounded like one pair of shoes instead of two.

I drove toward the city and found a parking place. We entered the big glass doors of Bergman's Department Store and ascended marble stairs to a cafe on the mezzanine. The red plastic covered booth felt icy cold as we slid into seats opposite each other. I ordered cokes. Marie sat across from me, propped on her knees, and sucked fizz through a straw. She blinked her eyes uncontrollably.

We stood by the balcony and watched herds of people. The tops of their heads moved like marbles spilled from a bag. We descended the stairs and joined the masses of Saturday shoppers.

I purchased one wardrobe for myself, and one for the child with me. I wanted everything to be new for us. I wanted to savor cutting the tags off of each article, and inhaling the aroma of virgin fabric. We bought shorts, shirts and hats, sandals and beach towels. Our shopping bags were packed with newness as we went from one department to another in the huge, elegant store. The process was hurried, but I felt that each purchase was taking us closer to our destination.

We opened the trunk of the dark green car, and placed everything inside. We settled into the automobile's long front seat. The inside of the car felt like protective padding to embrace us, and lift us away. I started the ignition and drove south, out of the dirty city.

Marie and I felt the wind in our hair and on our faces. She held her hands out of the window, as if to catch and hold onto freedom from the breeze.

Night fell, and we ordered sandwiches from a weathered shack of a restaurant. I didn't want to stop for the night. So I kept driving. Kept on heading south and waiting for the swaying blue-green palm trees to waved me into a place I knew we were supposed to be.

Marie was sleepy after her meal. As we continued our journey, she scooted very close to me. Her young, tender back leaned against my side. I stroked her velvety hair until she rested her head in my lap.

When Marie awoke, it was morning. She looked up at the sky, peeled her skin off of the car seat, and sat up. Her lungs seemed to open as she took a deep breath of salty air. She felt as if a soothing ointment was being spread over her by the hands of an angel.

Marie watched as I walked out of the hotel office. I held a key attached to a black key ring. Large white numbers identified our cabin.

I drove the car toward our temporary residence, and parked on a driveway covered in pebbles. Our tires crunched over the rocks and made popping sounds like milk on fresh Rice Krispies.

The cabin faced the ocean and was surrounded by palms, bushes, flowers. We entered a screened-in porch that smelled salty and fishie and wonderful.

Faded shells were scattered about, probably left by former visitors. I worked the key into the rusty lock and opened the front door. The living room invited us to become a part of the life there. Bamboo furniture was upholstered in bark cloth that held my eyes with its' soft patina. Shelves were stacked with dog-eared books.

Ceiling fans and floor fans were scattered throughout the cottage. I opened windows and the air became almost visible and liquid as it bathed our wrinkled clothing. Breezes brushed the perspiration off of our faces and hair.

Across from the living room, was a sunny windowed studio. It was empty except for a desk and chair. Marie followed me.

"We can do some artwork if you like," I said.

The child gave a slight smile.

A rustic room with two iron double beds awaited us. The beds were fresh with white linens and spreads.

Marie was blinking her eyes again. Her fear of being left was apparent. She worried that I would go in the night and never come back. I asked about her fear. "Why, Marie, do you think I would want to leave you?"

"Because I'm bad," she replied.

I tried to reassure her, but worry lines did not fade from her young face.

Marie's little soul had been tainted. I needed to nurture the child and show her the goodness in her nature. "Look at the Sea, Marie. Look at all it has to offer us."

I brought our bags inside, and begin to make a home. I placed our clothing in dresser drawers and arranged our toiletries in the bathroom. I opened the heavy trunk of the car and found art supplies. I spread them out in the windowed room.

Marie and I carried tall glasses of ice water and beach towels, out into the sun. The breeze lifted our towels and placed them onto the waiting sand. I realized my exhaustion, collapsed on the towel, and sunk deep into softness. I felt all of the tension go out of my muscles, while I listened to the music of birds and breaking waves. Marie was playing with her bucket and shovel. As I floated between waking and sleep, I knew that she would be alright. Nothing bad would happen to Marie.

I awoke slowly, with an uncommon feeling of rest-fulness and complete relaxation. Marie was close be-side me, intently working in the sand. I jumped up, grabbed her by the hand and the two of us ran toward the glorious waves of the ocean.

We played until we were tired and ravenously hun-gry. A nearby market provided fish, vegetables bread and fruit.

I cooked while Marie bathed and got into her paja-mas. We took our plates of food out onto the porch and saw the last fire-washed flicker of sunset. I lit candles in hurricane lamps. The darting glow gave our surround-ings a pleasant warmth.

Marie and I moved to the cushioned porch swing. I rocked the swing back and forth until Marie reclined and rested her head in my lap. She stretched her feet onto the chain and moved her small toes up and down the metal links. She sang softly and talked about the fun she had had. She anticipated the next day and wanted to make plans. Her sleepiness overtook her ex-citement as she drifted off. I watched her face, listened to her breathing and reflected upon my own childhood.

Each day was full of surprises and simple gifts. We utilized the "painter's studio," and praised each other's art. I had been an artist most of my life, but a child was showing me different ways to use the paint. She sug-gested new scenes and different perspectives. I showed her how to sprinkle salt into puddles of paint on paper. She enjoyed the results.

"Salt is healing, isn't it?" asked Marie.

"Yes," I answered.

Marie and I strolled along the boardwalk and talked with other vacationers. We ate cotton candy and rode the Ferris wheel. Marie played with other children. I was fascinated. I had forgotten how children connect immediately. How easily they make friends. They hung onto a big tire tube in the water. The waves were their roller coaster and they screamed with excitement. I found happiness in their spontaneity and jubilance.

Our last day was quietly relished. We spent most of our time on the beach, and gathered more shells for our collection. We examined each smooth, shiny form and named it's rich colors.

Over such a short period of time, Marie had changed. Outwardly she looked healthier. Her usually pale skin had turned a golden color and there were blonde streaks in her hair. She had gained weight and she had quit blinking her eyes. The nightmares had stopped. I told Marie how much she was loved. I told her over and over again.

When night fell, we crawled into our beds. We talked back and forth for a while, as we had done before. But on the last night, Marie slid out of her bed and crawled into mine. She snuggled against me. I patted her back and rubbed her head. I told her that we would have sweet dreams of stars sparkling on blue water. I told her a story about a ship that rocked a little girl to sleep, and when she awoke, she stepped into a land where nothing could hurt her.

My story entered our separate dreams, which flew through the night, and formed pictures to access or suppress.

Morning came and a jolt of energy caused me to jump out of bed. As I walked to the kitchen to make coffee, I realized that my chronic backache had eased. I went back into the bedroom and pulled my suitcase out from under the wicker bed. I stuffed my belongings into the bag, zipped it closed, pulled out the handle and rolled it onto the porch. I unplugged my laptop. How much time had I spent writing at that computer?!

I gathered up sheets of watercolor paper that were strewn around the sunroom. My paintings were lively and fresh. I hadn't realized it, but they were quite good. I rolled up the papers and secured them with a rubber band.

My red Honda looked drab from gathering a film of salty sea spray. "My word!" I had been here for two weeks!

I went into the bathroom and splashed water on my face. I examined my reflection in the mirror. Freckles! The sun had caused my freckles to come back. I hadn't noticed them since I was a kid. A kid with a Buster Brown bob and a face full of freckles. What do you know? I thought they had faded forever, under my daily ritual of sunscreen.

I felt invigorated as I poured a cup of steaming coffee. Still in my pajamas, I walked out to the edge of the water.

The time away was good. I felt like a child who had been set free. So many hurts in my past. Things were going to be okey. I was healing. I don't think it was an accident that I came to this place.

That day, two weeks ago, when I was driving aimlessly. Remembering something. Trying to come to terms with something. That awful rainy day. I sat in the car and looked at the old house. It had been renovated and turned into lawyers' offices.

I ran into a Wal-Mart to get some things. A few toiletries, jeans and T-shirts. The recollections were fuzzy and far away in my mind.

I placed my empty coffee cup in the sand and started running and jumping. I was a crazy fifty-eight year old woman, but who cared? I spun around in circles and lifted my hands to the sky. I created a dance of my own and sang to the top of my lungs.

"I'm Marie and I'm free! Like a bee, like the sea, like a bird in a tree. Let it go, let it be, lay it down, that's the key, Gee, look at me, I'm Marie and I'm free!"

A WINDOW OF TRUTH

We met at an exclusive resort. The company that our husbands worked for was holding one of it's frequent "party-conferences."

That day, when I first met Basil Edwards, the four of us went to lunch. Her red-headed husband and my red-headed husband were full of personality, so to speak, and did all of the talking.

I noticed Basil. She fingered her menu and slowly lifted her eyelids to reveal large beautiful blue eyes. She smiled at her husband, Burton as if she enjoyed his plethora of jokes as much as he did.

Basil was tall and thin, and her delicate features were framed by short, wispy blonde hair. Her clothes draped and melted into perfection, introducing a body made for quality design.

I sized her up, but was dead wrong. I would eventually find out that she was an avid reader, had an extensive vocabulary and was the wittiest woman I had ever known. I also discovered that she was humiliated by Burton's loud mouth and boring jokes.

Ruddy was going to be golfing and "conferring" all day. He invited me to go along and drive the cart. I had nothing better to do. Basil and I were unaware, at that point in time, that we shared miles of common ground. She stayed in her hotel room. If I had only known, I would have spent the day with her.

I have no interest in Golf. Hours of watching people whack a stick at a ball can become extremely monotonous. I admired the scenery and thought about the upcoming party that night. I looked forward to those parties, where a little wine warmed me and dissolved the reality of being married to a traveling man who liked women.

I was tired from sitting in the golf cart, so I exited to stretch and walk a bit. The green grass was tempting and I was still young and agile. I turned a cartwheel.

Then I turned another which was a fatal mistake. The earth soared straight toward me with magnificent force. I landed on my rear, passed out from pain and woke up in the emergency room of a strange hospital.

Upon waking, the first image in my mind was the party. What about my nice dress, admiring glances, wine? The injection made my legs go numb and my mind feel euphoric. By the time we returned to the hotel, the narcotic quickly changed directions.

I stumbled into the lobby, broke out in a cold sweat and proceeded to throw up.

I suppose Ruddy had a great time dancing to live music and flirting in the dim lights.

Several months later, Basil and I were invited to our husbands' business dinner at a restaurant in Nashville, Tennessee. We were both attractive women. Ruddy and Burton knew we were attention getters. We made them feel important while they viewed us as extensions of themselves. Charms to dangle, then drop and forget.

In that restaurant in Nashville, Tennessee, Basil and I scooted our chairs close together and began a bond that has lasted more than twenty years. We talked at the table and we excused ourselves to the ladies room numerous times.

Two good-looking abandoned women with anxiety attacks, depression and extensive wardrobes. We were empty yet full of our fleeting selves. Enjoying the only thing people knew about us, that we were outwardly beautiful.

As time passed and our friendship grew stronger, Basil and I discovered that a benefit of this connection was having ample time together. Time to dawdle at lunch, go shopping, drink wine in hotel rooms and talk, talk talk. Basil had three young children and I had two. We missed them terribly during these trips but we also wanted to be away. It was that "maternal pull" that most mothers feel. The wine helped.

We weren't necessarily attracted to business men but we thrived on their attractions to us. In our desperate conditions, we could see past objectionable appearances and behavior. We became adept at turning these men into objects of interest and fascination.

Basil and I continued to play out fantasies in our separate cities and neighborhoods. The man who came to fix the plumbing "bore a striking resemblance to a model in the J. Crew catalog." The woman next door "had a perfect husband an they had a perfect marriage." "All eyes were on us as we sashayed down the isles of our respective Piggly Wiggly's and Kroger's."

In New York City, Basil and I stood side by side looking through a wall of windows. We were at the top of a magnificent city and unaware, for a moment, of the mass of drunken humanity around us.

Were we seeing New York or our reflections in the window? Did we gaze upon the moon, dark sky and twinkling lights, or our long golden hair, and black dresses? We turned and walked into the crowd to receive our acclamations.

Ruddy called me one day and said we were moving to a city in the Midwest. Nothing was predictable with him. I cried and screamed and said I wasn't going. My older son was devastated. The younger one took it upon himself to make everything alright. Too large a task for a little boy. Ruddy traveled during the week. What difference did it make where his family lived?

The midwestern city was like a foreign country. My twelve year old threatened to run away from home. I said I'd go with him. The eleven year old utilized his training in the children's acting guild, and pretended everything was fine. I missed my job at the TV station so badly that I began watching soap operas just to be near a television. The snow piled up to the window sills and stayed for five months. Ruddy traveled more than ever.

After a year, the company moved us back to the south. I was thrilled and tired at the same time. Twelve moves, more painting and wallpapering, moving boxes and furniture. My back was beginning to ache. I was getting older. There were so many layers of different patterned wallpaper that I had carefully pasted in rooms to try and make a home. The colors and patterns attached themselves to my mind and I couldn't peel them off. So many tries at starting afresh and wanting to make it better.

Five or six years passed. Ruddy changed jobs, so the momentary glitter and glamour with Basil was gone. We still carried out our long distance relationship by telephone, letters and occasional visits. We made each other laugh and lived our lives eternally connected.

Years later, I looked through photographs from the New York trip. Basil was wearing a soft pink sweater and a felt hat. The wind on the little cruise boat was strong and she held onto her hat with a graceful hand. Ruddy and Burton were on either side of her, making ridiculous faces.

I carefully cut around the image of Basil. "Ruddy and Burton" were delegated to the trash can. I pasted the picture of Basil next to a picture of me and recreated history in my mind.

Ruddy and I took a walk in the park behind our farmhouse. It seemed like a typical week-end except for the knowledge that we would be moving again. I had been packing for weeks. The boys and I were emotionally resigned to living in yet another strange city. I would have to give up my job as a graphic artist but I could find another.

The walking track seemed the same, the trees, the familiar faces of walkers and runners.

The sounds of our feet on gravel were broken by a shocking decision that Ruddy verbalized. His words felt like gravel leaping off of the path and creating a tornado headed straight for me. Stinging, burning, small jagged edges tearing into my skin and heart.

"I don't think I can move y'all to Texas. It just wouldn't be right. I'm finding myself attracted to another woman." I thought the broken-record had long since silenced itself. I always knew through the years. I knew about Debbie and Carol and Mary and on and on. He always told me. Ruddy couldn't keep his mouth shut. He was worse than any woman I'd ever known.

No secret ever went from my lips to Ruddy's ears because it would come right out of his mouth for all to hear.

To answer the proverbial question directed at me: "Why did you stay so long?" I thought he would grow out of it. I thought he would get over them. I thought I couldn't make it on my own. I wanted to stay home with the boys while they were small. I didn't want to go to work and leave them with a stranger. Who knows why a woman does what she does? It's a matter of survival.

We kept walking. My heart was racing and my mouth was numb. But all I could utter, was, "Ruddy, you don't get to have another mid-life crisis. You have reached your limit."

On Monday, I made an appointment with a lawyer. The walk from my car to his office was long and terrifying.

Basil and I lost contact for a while. My new life was so wonderful that I forgot everything. I never dreamed I would meet someone and marry again. I was in my late forties. Andy was better than any fantasy I'd ever had about a repairman or the next-door neighbor's husband.

My sons are grown and married now. My husband and I are happy and solid. I'm glad I'm not gorgeous anymore. It's too much of a burden to bear.

I haven't seen Basil in years, but through the miracle of email we are part of each others' lives again. Sometimes we talk about the "good old days" though neither of us would have them back. Basil is a grandmother. Hard to imagine! She tells me she's fat but I seriously doubt it.

When we have that reunion we've been talking about, I don't think we will require a circle of eyes around us. We don't need it anymore. We'll face each other instead of our reflections in the big city window. And the night will turn to morning.

SHINBONE RIDGE

It was a hot morning in 1921. Henry awoke in his upstairs room and smelled his mother's cooking. His night-
shirt stuck to his small body, and his red hair was wet
from the heat. There was no breeze blowing through the
open windows. But seven-year old Henry was too excited to be concerned with physical discomfort. He
hopped out of bed and rushed down the stairs. His
mother placed a huge breakfast in front of him. He didn't
want to think about eating. Anticipation of the day and
night ahead made breakfast seem unimportant.

Henry's mother pointed her finger at the plate, so
he ate. His little sister giggled, because Henry was being forced to choke down eggs and bacon. He pulled
her hair, then ran upstairs as fast as he could. Blood
curdling screams followed, and he laughed out loud.

Henry, Irving, Clark and other Cub Scouts from
around town, were looking forward to heading for the
mountains. It wasn't going to be just any ordinary
campout. The big boys were in charge. Boy Scouts were
going to accompany the younger kids to the best camping place imaginable: Shinbone Ridge.

Shinbone Ridge was a mountainous region with
cool springs running over rocks and spilling into the
most wonderful swimming hole. The place was abun-
dant with caves and tall trees.

Henry was bursting with excitement as he gathered his gear and rolled up scratchy wool blankets for a bedroll. He had a canvas-covered metal canteen which would be filled repeatedly from the flowing springs at the ridge. Henry loved drinking outdoor water. It wasn't like the water at home. It tasted like tree bark, dirt and stones. Everything that appealed to a seven-year old boy.

The Boy Scouts, some of whom were sixteen and even older, were the leaders on this trip. Called to be "shining examples" in their roles as responsible guides. They had learned it all. First aid, life guard training, how to cook over a campfire, pitch tents and tie ropes into numerous knots with names.

At ten minutes until ten o' clock, Henry, Irving and Clark hoisted backpacks and bedrolls onto their backs, and walked over to the Methodist Church.

The Boy Scouts arrived in three vehicles, parked the cars and got out. They towered over the younger ones, in their height and their intimidations. They shouted orders and criticized rumpled uniforms. They were going hiking and camping, Henry thought to himself. Why did they have to look so spic and span?

Gear was loaded into one car and boys into the others. The drivers must have been speeding at thirty miles an hour! Fun and freedom ran through their veins.

The black Fords wound and bumped up the mountain. Boys talked and laughed while supplies bounced and rolled. Dust flew as the cars came to a stop, and boys scrambled out. But Henry's dreams of jumping right into that swimming hole were thwarted. The Boy Scouts had other plans, and their plans came first.

Sometimes Henry thought that being in the Scouts was a little too much like school. He didn't see the point in learning how to lay out a campfire or in knowing the names of trees. The boys ate sandwiches from sack lunches they brought and then tried to stay awake as the Boy Scouts demonstrated how to apply a tourniquet.

After lessons and lectures, it was finally time for their hike. The fruity smells of earth, pine needles and berries were pleasant and tempting. Henry wanted to take big bites out of nature and chew slowly.

Thirst reached the boys throats just about the time they heard the rushing sound of springs. Thirsty dry mouths and hot bodies were ready to taste and feel cool water.

The Boy Scouts gave themselves and their charges permission to plunge into the waiting pool. They ran, jumped, swung on vines and felt like they were flying as they dropped into the swimming hole. They dove, swam and floated on their backs while the Boy Scouts constantly counted heads.

The hike back to camp was slow and relaxed. Thankfully, nothing was said about naming leaves, trees and Poison Ivy.

Each boy was assigned a job for supper duty, but the older boys did most of the work. They dug a hole in the ground and placed coals from the fire in the bottom. A big pot of stew was set on top of the coals, covered with more coals, and then covered up with dirt.

It would be quite a while before time to eat. Waiting boys passed around hard boiled eggs and homemade cookies their mothers had slipped in their packs.

While the stew simmered, the smell of each ingredient intensified everyone's hunger pangs. But they sat on the ground and learned songs from the Boy Scout Songbook. The younger ones couldn't carry a tune, but it was the idea that mattered.

They learned how to tie a "square knot, half hitch and sheepshank." They were given other "survival" lessons while thinking about and waiting for the food.

Finally, Lawrence, the biggest Scout, lifted the huge iron pot out of the coals. He wrapped a rag around the handle and slowly set the pot on a flat rock. Metal plates and spoons rattled as the boys formed a line. They picked up slices of bread and canteens of water. One by one, each received a generous serving of stew. Even peas and carrots tasted good cooked outdoors.

A bucket of water had been heating over the fire in preparation for clean-up. After every last bite of supper was consumed, the boys halfway sloshed their plates and utensils in hot water. It was time for circling around the campfire, singing, "Row, Row, Row Your Boat" again, and hopefully hearing some good ghost stories.

The Cubs heard a few stories, but Henry and his buddies didn't think they were very scary. Then, Cecil Thurman, casually mentioned to the young boys, that they needed to be careful in the night. Cecil told them, "Do NOT leave this campsite under any circumstances!" He cleared his throat and put more emphasis behind the warning in his voice. "Do all of you understand me?"

Silence fell until Little Pete Roberts spoke up. "Why would you say all that, Cecil?"

"Uh, well, you see, Little Pete, I didn't really want to have to tell y'all this, but I might as well. There are bootleggers in these woods. A whole clan of 'em. They live up th' mountain in th' worst lookin' shack you could imagine. They make moonshine. They've got long beards, no teeth and they stink to high heaven! And, Little Pete an th' rest uv y'all — they've got guns!"

"Guns?!!!" the Cubs all shouted at once. "Shushhhh!" commanded the Boy Scouts. "Y'all want em ta hear you?" "Nooooo," seven little boys said very quietly and in unison.

Herbert Gilmore stood up, stretched, yawned and patted his pockets. "Hey, men, I'm gonna walk down to the cars. Think I'll get a cigarette. Anybody want one? I'm not talkin' about you little runts, ya hear? Y'all are too young for a man's recreation."

A couple of the Boy Scouts nodded, "yes," and Herbert took off down a dark trail. Henry, Irving, Clark, Robert, T.J., William and Little Pete looked at each other with wide eyes and pounding hearts.

Herbert was gone for half an hour before the leaders started acting worried. Floyd Hendrix spoke first, "Hey, what you boys think? Think something's happened to Herbert?" "I don't know, Pal," said Dawson Barnes, "I think I'd better go look for him." "No," said Lawrence. "There's no denying I'm the biggest one of y'all. I'll go." Lawrence slowly lifted himself up, turned around and headed into the dark. His heavy feet crunched through sticks and pine cones.

Too much time was passing. They sang more songs and tried to tell scary stories. But nothing was fun anymore. Henry wished he was back in his bed at home. He would rather eat five plates of bacon and eggs than be in a mountain full of bootleggers. He even missed his sister. Things were really bad.

Cecil reached for one of the lanterns beside the campfire. He stood up, and lifted it high. He moved it around until the light caught sight of something. The young boys saw the startling image. They screamed, and ran wildly into their tents.

Seven year old Clark Evans fell to his knees and started praying the Lord's Prayer. He called out to Jesus and begged for a miracle to save them. They were all crying and yelling for their mamas.

Henry and several others peeped out of their tents and saw him coming. Herbert was covered in blood. What he was saying was barely audible. "Th' bootleggers!! They got me! Th' bootleggers!"

Herbert fell to the ground. Clark was still praying, and some of the others were making promises to God. They would "never be bad again," they'd "do anything their parents said." It was awful! It was the end.

Cecil and Dawson bent over Herbert. Vernon Moss screamed to the young boys, "Stay in your tents! Th' bootleggers are coming!" Henry just wanted to go ahead and die right there. Mostly he wanted to wake up from the awful nightmare.

Cecil and Dawson couldn't contain themselves any longer. They burst out laughing; holding their stomachs. Lawrence lumbered out of the woods with a wet towel. Herbert stood up, grabbed the towel and wiped ketchup off of his face, arms and torn clothes.

The Cubs wanted to be mad at their "shining examples." It had been a dirty prank. But they had been through fear like they'd never known. It was all over, and, now, for some strange reason, they felt a little more grown up.

They were privy to what big boys do. They even felt sort of proud to be part of it all. Irving said he "knew it was fake the whole time." The Cub Scouts were on the road to becoming men.

Both groups of boys, the young and the older, sat around the campfire and laughed long into the night.

THE DANCE

I'm happy that I danced with him when he was eighty-seven. The ship rocked softly. The waves were smooth, like his dancing, and as easy as our love for each other.

He smelled fresh, like tropical breezes, and his white hair shone in the festive lights. His suit was crisp where my left hand rested on his shoulder.

The music floated onto the dance floor, up through our toes and into two minds that loved the beauty of rhythm. He showed me the "old University steps" and I followed along.

We had been dancing together since he picked me up and twirled me around the rooms of our little house. I grew to "knee-high" and stood on his feet. We waltzed until I became older and too heavy to perch on his shiny shoes.

He saw his grandsons twirl their wives to Big Band music and recreate the steps he learned as a young man. He watched and remembered as they repeated the same moves, turns and swings that he knew by heart.

He reached for Mama's small frail hand and led her onto the floor. He held her tightly as they moved to the music. The last voyage on the vast ocean, and the last dance.

I can still feel my small feet on top of his. I long to follow his gentle lead as I look up, see his face and dance to the rhythms of life.

INTERVENTION

The 1980's Honda Accord was old. But it was Joe's first car, affordable and mostly reliable. When something went wrong, Ed and Joe would spend hours under the hood or with their legs sticking out from under the chassis.

Ed taught Joe a lot about working on cars. Especially during that summer when both of the boys lived with us.

Brice and Joe were enrolled in separate colleges and decided to apply for jobs close to our hometown in Alabama.

Brice was studying communications and acquired a position as an intern at the TV station where his stepdad worked. Ed was thrilled about having his son ride to and from work with him and being able to engage in "TV talk."

Joe was the financial wizard who's major was German and International Business. So, he worked as a teller at a bank.

As their mother, I was in my element having both of my sons for a summer. Their past activities included summer school, or studying in a foreign country, or working in some other city and living with a bunch of guys.

Understandably, the weekends were a time for Brice and Joe to take off to Nashville and party with old high school friends. Occasionally, we'd host a "house party" and Nashville would come to them. We had a hot tub, which was an attraction, and enough room for the gang to spread out and find places to "crash."

One particular Saturday, we waved good-bye as the boys took off in their separate cars. Brice was following Joe.

There is something about the ringing of a telephone that can sound exciting or ominous. The ring that came about thirty minutes after the boys left, caused my heart to leap in my throat. A mother's intuition, I guess.

"Mom, I'm ok," was the first thing Joe said. Both sons have understood me long enough to use those words before any other utterance. I breathed a sigh of relief. "But the car went dead and we're parked on the side of the interstate, one exit up." We'll be there in ten minutes," was my response. Cell phones were unheard of at that time, so they had walked to a gas station pay phone.

Ed carried everything in his toolbox. So, we took off in his truck. There they were, the two of them standing in the hot sun with the Honda hood propped open.

Ed examined the inner workings of Joe's old car and evaluated the situation. He knew right away that a spark wasn't getting to the distributor and that he needed a coil wire to get it going. The one thing that Ed didn't have was the wire.

I was standing back away from the process when I felt a little red truck beside me. I felt it as if it were a breeze. I never heard it drive up or stop and I didn't see it coming. A man got out and walked toward my family of consulters and inspectors.

"Having some trouble?" or some such question was all that he asked. He didn't make conversation, but glanced under the hood and walked to his truck. He came back to the car, holding a coil wire in his hand. Then, he leaned into the motor and attached the wire in the right position. The man who seemed to come out of nowhere, worked fast. It was done in a split second and Joe's car started immediately.

We were all a little stunned. Ed thanked him profusely and asked if he could pay him something. His answer still comes to me when I'm not really thinking about anything. He said, "No, just stop and help someone in a little red truck sometime."

The red truck made a drastic U-turn across the median. I watched because I wanted to follow him with my eyes. The truck vanished. It disappeared into thin air. It was gone! Ed saw it too. But the boys were preoccupied with getting to their destination.

We told our sons good-bye once again and drove home in a state of mental impact and wonder. We talked about the incident over and over. We tried to question our eyes, our perceptions. But the same answer kept coming back and haunting us.

About a year later, Ed was driving home from work in his usual uneventful way. He had worked at the TV station for over twenty years, and the thirty minute commute was memorized and repetitive. But on that particular day, he glanced over to the side of the interstate and saw a man standing outside of a little red truck.

Ed pulled over and the man gratefully entered the passenger's side of his vehicle.

The two men introduced themselves, discussed the problem with the truck and headed for an auto parts store. But then, the stranger's conversation turned and became different from the usual "man-sports-weather" talk. He told Ed the story of his life and the changes he had made for the better.

After spending some time in the parts store, Ed drove the man back to his stalled red truck. They gave each other a farewell wave and Ed told him to call if he needed any more help.

The remainder of Ed's drive home was not rote or mundane. Something important had been fulfilled and he knew beyond a shadow of a doubt, that coincidence was not a factor.

IT HAPPENED LIKE THIS:

He didn't tell me much. I had to initiate conversation, and when I did ask questions, he answered with, "yes," or "no." It was a downright strain having him sit there. I don't know why in the world he wanted to come into my cramped little office. It was the size of a walk-in closet, and I had to share it with my supervisor, Rob.

Rob was a large man who talked on the phone to his wife at least ten times a day. I was glad that he was so in love with her, but I was also, envious. My own marriage was on a downhill slide, and my husband made it clear that I was a low priority.

When Rob was out of "our" office, Eddie would slide right in and sit in a chair beside my drafting table. I finally figured out that he was hiding from anyone who might want him to do something. He was right up under my nose, and was so quiet, that it made me extremely uncomfortable.

Eddie didn't seem uncomfortable, though. He seemed perfectly happy to just sit there and say nothing. I went through the usual "getting to know you" litany. "Now, where did you say you're from? Where did you say you went to college?"

I had recently started the job and it was the most exciting time of my life. Working took my mind off of my troubles, and brought in some much needed money.

I was thirty-five years old and my sons, Brice and Joe, were old enough to stay alone until I got home. The pay wasn't all that great, but the glamour made my heart beat with anticipation.

Every morning, as I dressed and brushed my long, 1970's hair, I looked forward to being THE artist for a CBS affiliate television station. Not only was my artwork seen on the air, but I had the opportunity to meet a multitude of TV stars.

On a trip to Atlanta, I spent thirty minutes in the same room with Tom Selleck. I brought him a coke and wrote out cue cards so he could tell all of north Alabama and Tennessee, how great channel 19 was. He looked into the camera with that beautiful face, and invited everybody to "watch Magnum P.I." Tom Selleck wasn't all that famous then, and he's back to being not so famous now. Most young people have probably never heard of him.

As far as I was concerned, I was working in New York City, instead of Huntsville, Alabama, in a little bitty TV station down the street from my house.

I occasionally "went out on assignment" to do courtroom art. I traveled to nearby cities and drew pictures of vile murderers and crooked politicians.

I was in my element and experiencing the first "dream job" I had ever had.

An artist needs space. Time to think of ideas and create. There were no computers in those days, so I drew everything by hand and cut and pasted every piece of lettering. It was a time consuming occupation.

It was hard enough when Rob was in the confining space with me, but somehow, it was worse when Eddie was there. At least Rob shuffled papers, talked to his wife and shuffled more papers. Then he'd jump up, go out into the common area and start yelling at people. Rob didn't seem to notice I was around.

But Eddie Parker was quite a study. He was perplexing. He was a young man, about nine years my junior, and had never been married. He was average in height and build, and was handsome in a boyish kind of way. He had dark hair that looked as if it was combed by his mama everyday before work. He had a dark beard, and a bright toothy smile, that he flashed frequently.

Eddie had beautiful green eyes, that were unfortunately rimmed in red every morning. I surmised that he had quite a social life and wondered how he could keep it up all week long. But he was young.

Eddie's job at the TV station, was commercial production. He went out with a heavy video camera, and tried to make business owner's daughters look good. He came back to the station and edited everything together so that the client would be pleased. I later learned how very talented this young man was. And I learned that there was more to him than his puffy red eyes told me.

In between getting art ready for the "world to see," I found out bits and pieces about the strange boy who didn't seem to have any social skills. He came from a family of mostly women. That explained his inability to converse. They did his talking for him.

Eddie's parents had four children. His older brother was married, and his father often worked at night. So, he was surrounded by a mother, two sisters, grown nieces, aunts and female cousins. And the most bizarre thing, was that they all lived in the same neighborhood. Even Eddie's "bachelor apartment" was down the street from his parents.

I began to form a picture in my mind. "The Waltons" was a television show which was popular around that time. A family of about ten people lived in a huge house, and they all loved each other. Parents, kids, grandparents. They kept up with each other's every move and they all told each other "good-night" through the walls of the old farm house. Eddie's family used the telephone to call and tell each member "good-night."

The Parker family piled around a large kitchen table at least once a week and ate together. Eddie's mama did all of the cooking for fifteen to twenty people. The whole idea made me feel sick and claustrophobic. I was an only child and had very few relatives. I was a private person and didn't want my family knowing everything I did. Eddie didn't seem to mind that they knew his business.

Eddie really loved his mother. I began to wonder if he was a "mama's boy." Maybe the red eyes were from crying because he had to leave her and go to work. I had much more to do than try and figure that boy out. But, he continued to sit in my office.

Eventually, I found out that Eddie was in love with Julie. He didn't tell me in so many words. He just began to talk about her. He was covert, but women have a knack for intuiting and fitting the puzzles together. He was desperately in love with that girl, and would have married her in a heartbeat.

But, Julie wanted to be "just friends." So, Eddie took what he could get, in hopes that someday she would look at him in a different way. He raced home from work in his little convertible, and anticipated a phone call or visit from Julie.

One day, my car battery went dead. Eddie got his cables, hooked them from his car to mine, and I was going in no time. I learned that he could pull an entire engine out of a vehicle, take it apart and put it back together again. He knew all about mechanical stuff and all about electronics. Eddie didn't brag about his abilities. They just came naturally to him. He was a humble person and had a sweet spirit. Eddie's persona began to radiate around my cramped quarters and I became more comfortable with the absence of words between us.

I knew that Eddie would help me if I had car trouble, and I knew that he would make the hour's drive from his house to mine if I ever needed him for anything. I knew I had a friend and it was a nice, warm feeling. But I still thought he was immature in some ways, and had horrible taste in music.

After I had worked at channel 19 for about a year, I became part of a "surrogate family." Lots of good friends to talk to and share my innermost concerns with. I found people who were willing to listen to me and who seemed to like me the way I was. I joined the "after work crowd" and felt very "big city." About once a week, we'd gather at a local trendy spot and act obnoxious with our loud laughter and raucous behavior.

In 1982, my world came crashing down. My husband, who traveled all week and some weekends, had accepted a transfer to the midwest. I was devastated, and even thought about staying behind. But, I considered that the move might give us a fresh start and put new life in our failing marriage. So, the four of us packed up and went.

Saying "good-bye" to my family of friends at work was horrible. I cried for days. We moved into a house in the new city and I cried for weeks. I cried as I pulled up carpet, painted and wallpapered rooms and listened to sad songs on the radio.

I ran up excessive telephone bills because I called my friends back home so much. But those friends had to get on with their lives. They couldn't listen to me forever. They couldn't fix it. Eddie had the ability to fix anything in the physical world, but he could not fix me. He could be sweet and quiet and listen, but he had no answers. His silence became uncomfortable again, because his presence wasn't there.

After pounding the streets for months, I eventually began to get freelance artwork. Back in Alabama, I had enjoyed pretending that I was "big city." But the raw fact of living in a real big city was not glamorous. It was noisy and dirty. I got lost on the interstate more times than I could count. I had anxiety attacks on the way to job interviews, while eighteen-wheelers blew dirt and rocks into my windshield. I longed for the little television station, and the comfort of friends.

We were eventually transferred back to the south. Nashville, Tennessee. I was lonely and disoriented, but glad to be back in more familiar territory. My two sons were my best friends. They were wonderful, but they couldn't be my constant companions. They had to adjust to a new place and make new friends. I hoped and prayed that we could stay put for a long while.

I didn't hear from my old friends much anymore. The "dream job" was a memory that was becoming less painful. Television stations are transient anyway. Many people move on to different markets. The old "family group" probably wasn't even there anymore. I wondered if Julie ever woke up and realized what a prize she could have in Eddie.

The marriage ended. My husband fell in love again, and I just told him to go off into the sunset with her. I was tired.

My sons and I stayed in Nashville, but moved into a brand new house. I put a swing out on the porch and sat there with my ice tea. There were nice neighbors around. I did courtroom art for a Nashville television station and then got a job at a screen print shop.

About once a month, I traveled three hours south, to visit with my parents. On the return trip from one of those visits, I was driving along in my usual daze, listening to island music.

Years before, Eddie Parker had introduced me to the music of Jimmy Buffett. At first, when he talked about being a fan, and going to concerts, I thought it was just one of many "generation gap moments" we'd had. But the more I listened to Jimmy, the more I liked his music. I discovered that Jimmy Buffett wasn't all that young. He was my age, and he sang about things I loved. Palm trees, the sea and life in the tropics.

So, as I was listening to Jimmy, I thought about Eddie. I wondered what he was doing with his life. If he had gotten married. I knew he had finally moved away from his parents' neighborhood. He'd bought a woodsy lot in the country and built a small house. I thought that was a mature move on his part.

It was as if the car just automatically pulled into an old run-down gas station and drove up to a phone booth that was set in the dirt in front of a bushy plot of land. I sat there, listening to Jimmy and looking at the telephone booth.

I dug in my purse and found my small, well-worn book of telephone numbers. P——, Packson, Palmer, Parker. I found a quarter, among chewing gum, lipstick and tissues. I opened the creaky door to the car I'd been left with in the divorce settlement. It had been a company car and the mileage was up to about two hundred thousand. The motor was in bad shape and I wondered how much longer it would last. I wondered if Eddie Parker could make it like new again.

One ring, two rings. "Hello, Eddie?" "Yeah." "This is Janet. I was passing through and thought I'd give you a call." "Hey!" he said. He sounded pleased to hear my voice. I asked him what was new.

"Well, I bought uh truck and I'm datin' somebody."

He asked what I'd been up to.

"I made a trip out to Seattle, I'm working at a screen print shop, Mama's been sick and I went to see her, I got a divorce."

I think I made an impact, because after a long silence, he asked me to repeat all of those things. I did. His passive nature had been shaken. There was no doubt about it. I had never heard such shock in Eddie's voice. He stammered and struggled for words.

Two months later, I got a birthday card in the mail. It was from Eddie. It was some kind of silly card that his mother had probably found at a flea market. At the bottom, he wrote, "Call me sometime, if you want to, Eddie."

I couldn't get to the telephone fast enough. I had to get him up to Nashville to fix my car!

My car wasn't broken down every weekend. But I surely was glad to see Eddie Parker's face at my front door. He told the girlfriend, "good-bye," and started getting a motel room in Nashville every Friday night.

I considered inviting him to stay at our house, but I didn't think the boys were ready for a male guest. Anyway, I thought it was good training for Eddie to pay for a room. He needed to quit being so "cheap."

The more time Eddie and I spent together, the narrower our age difference became. I think that happens when you get older. At the television station, back in the seventies, Eddie was twenty-six and I was thirty-five. We were worlds apart in our ages and our lifestyles. But time can close the gap.

We went to Jimmy Buffett concerts and took long hikes in the woods. We had picnics and went to antique stores. We became regulars at The Bluebird Cafe. We listened to country music singers who later became famous. I found out that Eddie loved all kinds of music and that our tastes were similar, after all. But, he still listened to his "southern rock" while he drove back to Alabama on Sundays, and I listened to Donna Summer by myself during the week.

Eddie talked. But I talked more, and Eddie listened. He hugged me and sat with me while I opened up one trunk full of "divorce baggage"after another. He listened to all of the garbage and blaming and the crying. But he didn't seem to mind. He just comforted me, and his sweet spirit radiated around me, like it did in that little cramped office at the TV station.

I finally realized and accepted the feelings I had carried around for years. I had loved Eddie Parker for a very long time. I loved him when his eyes were red, when he sat next to my drafting table. I loved him when he was too quiet, and while he was infatuated with Julie. Deep in my secret heart, I had wished for a caring man like Eddie. It was more than his ability to "fix" things. It was the way he loved his mother and sisters, and the good friend he was to so many people.

But the most astounding thing of all, was, that nothing was wrong with Eddie because he didn't date. He had gotten over Julie long before, and was waiting for me. He was knowingly, quietly waiting. I had no idea. I couldn't imagine that I was worth that kind of love. I felt like I didn't deserve him. Then he had to listen to me cry and carry on about how I wasn't good enough for him. But I got over it.

I was in my mid-forties during this time in my life. I just couldn't bring myself to say that I was "dating" someone. So, I suppose Eddie and I "spent time together" for about three years.

We talked often about marriage. And I guess we both just assumed we would make the big move after my younger son, Joe graduated from high school. But Eddie never "officially" proposed.

I probably didn't have enough to complain about, since being with Eddie was just about perfect. So, I started to feel sorry for myself because he hadn't proposed. One weekend, while I was in Alabama, I sat with Eddie at his kitchen table. Joe was six months away from graduating, but I was tired of "our companionship arrangement." So, I proposed to Eddie.

He answered with, "sure. When do you want to do it?"

I told him, "next weekend."

He was slightly taken aback, but said, "ok." I told him that I would line up the preacher and buy myself a "tropical wedding dress."

We sat there and stared at each other for a while. I told Eddie that we needed to buy some wedding rings. "Well, can't we just do that later on?" he asked. "No!" I replied emphatically. We've got to go right now and buy two wedding rings. Eddie had come a long way when it came to letting go of some of his money. And I had learned to translate the word, "cheap" into "conservative," but "cheap" with a capital "C" was rearing it's ugly head again.

We walked silently to Eddie's truck and headed for Service Merchandise. My ring was nothing to brag about, but at least it would communicate to other people that I was a married woman. I'd talk him into something better, later.

"A suit?!" It was all just too much for Eddie, who was accustomed to purchasing video and audio equipment. He didn't have to dress up for work, therefore, he didn't own a suit. I drug him to the Burlington Coat Factory and he darn well bought a suit, white shirt, tie, belt, dark socks and shoes.

After I had blurted out "next weekend" to Eddie, I remembered that I'd already planned a yard sale for Saturday and even placed an ad in the paper. But that was ok. We'd get married on Friday night and have the yard sale on Saturday.

Back home in Nashville, I told no one but the boys. They were excited and happy for me. They had formed a close bond with Eddie and enjoyed his automotive and electronic talents.

The week seemed endless. I thought Friday would never come. I was bouncing off the walls.

Eddie and I had been attending a church where hundreds of country music people went. We loved the music and the relaxed, casual atmosphere. People wore jeans and T-shirts and fellowshipped in the isles.

Neither of us had been drawn to stiff, ritualistic churches like the ones we had grown up attending. So, we just didn't go. That is, until we discovered the radical services that were being held at Christ Community in Franklin, Tennessee. So, that's where we wanted to get married.

I called the preacher and arranged a 6:30 ceremony. I bought a colorful, floral dress, and got things ready for the yard sale. Eddie and I talked on the phone at least four times a day, everyday.

I was terrified that something would happen and Eddie wouldn't make it on time. I was afraid he would be in an accident. I obsessed and worked myself into a frenzy. Eddie worked at the TV station until noon on Friday. Then headed for Nashville and made it just fine. We went to purchase our marriage license, came back and waited for the boys to get home from school.

Around four o'clock, the doorbell rang. Two women had parked their truck in the driveway, and were anxious to pilfer through our sale items a day early. We told them we had to go get married, but they didn't believe us.

So, we opened up the garage door and let them have at it. They piled half of our stuff into their truck and still wouldn't leave. I finally got the marriage license and shoved it in front of their faces. I said, "We have got to leave in an hour to go to the church and get married! You can come back tomorrow morning.

We went inside the house and decided it was time. I called my parents and told them that Eddie and I would be getting married that night. They were thrilled. My mother had been embarrassed about telling her friends that her forty-five year-old daughter had a "boyfriend." Then, Eddie called his parents. Eddie's mother and I had connected immediately after we met. I was crazy about the woman who had raised such a fine son.

All Eddie's mama had to do was call the beauty shop where Eddie's sister was having her hair done. Within fifteen minutes, all of Hartselle, Alabama knew that the confirmed bachelor was getting ready to alter his life forever.

Brice, Joe and Eddie looked so handsome in their suits. I wanted to cry, but didn't, for fear of having mascara streaked down my face. We got to the church in plenty of time for Eddie to set up his lights, white umbrella and tripod with video camera. The minister looked startled as he walked into the chapel. He must have thought it was all a joke and he was on Candid Camera.

But it was for real, although I couldn't believe it. My mind floated back to 1979 and the first time I saw Eddie Parker. Never in a million years would I have thought I'd ever be married to that boy. Life is full of surprises.

Our "reception" was dinner at our favorite restaurant in Franklin. Our guests were teenage friends of the boys. A musician came to our table and played the accordion. We had a ball. We had a little too much wine, and we had to get up at the crack of dawn, for a yard sale.

Our six month long-distance marriage was much better than long-distance "dating." I stayed in Nashville and waited for Joe to graduate from high school and head for college. Eddie and I took turns spending weekends at our Alabama and Tennessee homes.

The more time I spent at Eddie's house, the more I saw what was going to HAVE to go. His home was a cozy place with a living room, two bedrooms, kitchen and screened-in back porch. And his decor was just fine for his cozy little place. But not for "our" future home, in my estimation.

I looked at the large Jack Daniels barrel in the middle of the kitchen. The horse collar mirror hanging on the wall, and brick and board bookshelves. I was repulsed by gigantic speakers and a nasty recliner that Eddie had nested in for years. This wasn't going to be easy.

Eddie and I had been good friends before we had been anything else. I guess that's why we never had a disagreement. In all the years I had known him, we had never once had an argument. Not until I brought up the way I felt about "his stuff."

Eddie got mad. I had never seen him mad. But, Eddie Parker's "mad" is unique to Eddie. He gets his feelings hurt and he gets a little snippy. That's about the extent of it. He doesn't yell or stomp around. But I'd almost rather have seen him throw a fit than be hurt by my criticism of his stuff.

So, I decided to just let it lie for a while. After all, it would be several months before I moved to Alabama. I would have to sell my house, he would sell his, then we'd rent something while our rustic house on the hill was being built.

For ten years, Eddie had owned a beautiful piece of property on the side of a mountain. Thankfully, he didn't build the one-room log cabin he had been planning before we hooked up. The land was just sitting there, waiting for us to put down roots.

We both liked rustic, so that wasn't a problem. I've never been a "ruffles and lace" type of girl, but I do appreciate good furniture and tasteful design. Eddie had made some good choices at yard sales and junk stores, so some of his stuff would work fine. But, ninety percent of it would not.

Three months later, Eddie informed me that he wanted to have a yard sale at his house. I said, "fine. It'll be fun." I was amazed at how much he got rid of. Eddie had to make the decision for himself. He had to be the one to choose to get rid of the barrels, Early American sofa, and waterbed.

It all worked out, and the horse collar mirror looks great in our garage over the utility sink.

Eddie and I have been married for thirteen years, now. The best years of my life. The age difference is hardly noticeable anymore. We've forgotten what was going on in our lives when I was old enough to be his babysitter, or when he was in junior high school and I was bearing children. His dark hair and beard have turned gray. He is very distinguished looking, and his eyes aren't red anymore.

Brice and Joe are happily married now. Brice and his wife just became parents to a baby girl.

Eddie said to me, "Thank you for making me a grandfather." "Thank you for waiting for me," I answered. "You're the man of my dreams."

SHOOTIN' POOL

Daddy always wanted a pool table. He talked about it for years. There was absolutely no room for a pool table in the first little house we lived in. There really wasn't much room in the second house, either, but he broke down and got one.

I never knew the story behind his desire for the big green table with colorful balls. It could have been a throwback from his fraternity days at the University. He never mentioned the reason for wanting to have the game as part of his life.

We had a room off of the kitchen, and that's where the pool table went. It was supposed to be a "den," but my parents let me call it a "playroom." The Brittain kids had a huge playroom converted from a garage. They could play baseball in theirs. But there were four Brittain kids and only one of me, so I thought I should be satisfied.

I played records on my portable record player and danced around in there. I also used it as an art studio. There was an ancient upright piano in one corner and the only thing it was good for was to prop my drawing board on. I spread out my pastels on the top, which always stayed closed, sat on the piano bench and spent hours making art on the piano.

So, the Pool table was delivered and set up in the "playroom." I didn't mind because I was sixteen years old by then. Just so there was still room for the piano which held my art supplies.

I had always associated the game of Pool with the forbidden. Something girls weren't allowed to do. Boys were supposed to be eighteen before they could enter the dark mysterious doors in downtown Oneonta. Our town was small, but we had at least three Pool halls on main street.

I knew that some of the boys in my class frequented the halls even though they were under age. It was rumored that Bobby Hyde was quite a "shark."

I got familiar with the Pool table in our playroom. The more familiar I became with it, the more it seemed natural to me. I liked the cue stick and the feel of baby powder smoothed on it's surface. I liked the blue chalk and the way it made a difference when the stick tapped the white ball.

I learned about putting the "English" on the cue ball and Daddy taught me several games. I could put a spin on the ball so that I didn't scratch so often. I racked up the balls in the triangular wooden form and used the muscles I had developed at Girl Scout camp to put force behind the break. I neglected my homework and hung around that pool table after school everyday.

Popularity was not my strong suit. I had a few friends, but I wasn't part of the "in crowd." Boys were friendly enough to me, but didn't want to date me. Ronnie Allred told me that I just wasn't "a regular girl." I asked him what he meant and he replied with, "well, you don't flirt ner nothin'." So, I stayed to myself and refined my game of pool.

One day during lunch period, I mentioned to a friend that my daddy had bought a Pool table. Word spread like wildfire. But nobody believed me.

That afternoon, Mama picked me up from school as usual. We stopped by the grocery store and did a few more errands. We drove toward Shuff Mountain and made the daily ascent to our home. We wound up our steep, S-shaped driveway and discovered a dramatic difference in my quiet unassuming life.

There, at the top of our drive, were three cars and twenty-five kids. Music was playing from car radios and kids were jabbering and laughing. They sat in and on old souped-up cars and on the retaining wall behind our house.

The girls' full skirts were blowing in the mountain breeze as they bounced their feet to sounds of Elvis and Buddy Holley. They were not waiting for me. They were waiting to see the Pool table.

We didn't keep more than four or five Cokes at our house because I was the only one who drank them. One bag of potato chips, a small jar of peanut butter. Our house was not "stocked" for impromptu guests.

Teenagers didn't drop by, pop in and out, hang around. I was not a drawing card, but my daddy's pool table was. Things were changing. I'd take friends anyway I could get them. They all lined up and came in the back door.

There, before them, was the truth that they hadn't believed. All spread out in green felt and topped with numbered balls. The girls mostly just giggled and flitted around the boys. But the boys were ecstatic. They took turns getting serious about the game.

The crowds came everyday, but eventually dwindled down to just boys who wanted to improve their shots without paying by the hour. I finally decided it was time to stop sitting back. I decided to show the boys what I could do.

Some of them beat me, but not bad. Since I wasn't date material, they didn't "let" me win. After several rounds of Rotation, I was up against Bobby Hyde, the shark.

Bobby had cold black hair and was a large boy. He looked like a young Jackie Gleason. Bobby was witty, a popular guy and a football player. He was serious about his Pool.

The thing I remember the most, is Bobby putting down his cue stick and reaching out his hand to shake mine. It all plays out in slow motion in my mind. When I think about it, I like to make the scene last. To relive my feeling of confidence and accomplishment.

Bobby is walking toward me with his face a little flushed. His shiny black hair slightly flopped over one side of his forehead. He says, "Good game, Brice. Congratulations."

I had just experienced my finest hour, my fifteen minutes of fame and glory. I had beaten the shark.

SPECIAL DELIVERY

They come on a regular basis, yet I don't spend time dreading their arrival as much as I used to. There are too many things going on in my life to dwell on a possible emotional setback. But when I trudge down the long driveway from our hillside house to the big black mailbox, I often discover the unavoidable packets, that are dressed "fit to kill."

The colorful advertisements are printed on quality stock with a richness and shine that call forth images of a well-polished ship. The thick paper has a newness about it and an aromatic gift-like composition. Enticing photographs are wrapped and waiting for those with a wanderlust spirit. So, I am faced with the feelings that these luring packets evoke.

I choose not to open them while my dog and I tackle the incline. I stuff them under catalogs and other mail. A good monthly decorating magazine takes the sting and the edge off of the inevitable.

I will eventually examine the brochures. I'll open them and pour over every word, picture and colorful map.

I could throw them away upon arrival I suppose, but I'm never ready for such a drastic disposal. I cannot delegate them to the trash bin because I must go back in my memory and I must go forward with my healing.

The beautiful "invitations" to faraway places, address the past, so I allow myself the pain and pleasure of remembering.

I close my eyes and see you standing by the bridge. You're dressed in crisp white from your hat to your deck shoes. You were the "bridge" that held us together. You made the plans, filled out the forms, paid our fares and welcomed us aboard. You, my father, traveled the world.

We didn't always join you when you went to castles in England and seas that called to you on the spur of the moment. But often you said to us, "Let's go. Let's get away from this cold and sail where it's warm.

You were a seasoned traveler and knew how to pack. The rest of us didn't follow your example. We never learned to live minimally. "Don't take too much stuff. Unnecessary items hinder and burden, especially when you're rushing to catch trains."

When we joined you, we were privy to your lively personality and dry wit. You walked the length of the ship everyday. You sat in a deck chair looking from the sea to your John Grisham book. You read books and the sea and breathed in knowledge.

You lived in the present, although you had experienced eighty-six years. We joined you in the evenings, dressed for dinner and dancing. You asked each of us questions about our lives. Deliberate interest and a solid memory shone through your crystal blue eyes.

As I pour over the brochure pictures, I long for places I've never been. I smell salt air and hear the swaying palm trees. I know the roar of the ocean because you taught me to love it. I hear night trains and the soulful, soothing rocking of a berth. I imagine the sound of crumpling fresh sheets around me and the feel of a soft pillow on which to lay my head.

The address label spells out your name with letters that blur together. But maybe someday. Maybe someday we'll leave at a moment's notice. You won't be there, but we all have parts of you in us. Maybe someday, when the letters on the address label fall into place and I can read them with dry eyes.

THE GARDENER

Wooden boards on the back porch were trampled with awakening feet, bodies, minds. Creaky screen door, especially ordered for that country affect, slammed as boys juggled books and opened car doors.

The farmhouse table revealed luscious reds and greens. Santa Claus surprises on hot summer mornings. Tomatoes surrounded by home grown lettuce.

We might not see him for days. Or, we might catch a glimpse of fast moving, stark white hair, tanned skin, bare feet. Overalls, plaid shirt and a hand reaching up to wave.

There were flower days, too. And washed greens, shelled peas. Evidence of goodness beyond goodness, caring beyond caring.

The overgrown grass in our front yard disappeared. Daily newspapers traveled down the long driveway and rested on our back steps.

I was running late for my job in town. Dashing, brushing, frustrated. Door slamming so hard, it forgot to creak.

Startled, I saw him beside the large Oak tree.

"Oh, Mr. Inman! I didn't know you were there." Early morning sunlight and a soft breeze, cast animated shadows across his slender frame.

"Where ya been so long?"

"Oh, I'm a working girl, now. The divorce, you know."

"Well, we miss you. Come over to see us."

"I will. I get home late, and the boys need..."

"I'm not doin' too well" he said. "They won't let me live and they won't let me die."

A tired, sad, knowing face pierced my heart. He was tall, in spite of his age. I looked up at him. My arms reached out to embrace eighty years of strength, perseverance, compassion.

He said he was prepared to go. I was not prepared to lose him.

I fought the pain. I cursed, prayed and cried, as he walked back down my long driveway.

He turned back, smiled and waved.

ROYCE'S ACADEMY

"I don't know why in the world that boy is so anxious to go, do you, Henderson? He can't possibly get by with the tricks he pulls around here. Having to get up early and study late at night?! Why, he'll never do it! That son of yours will never make it."

Massie O'Reilly wasn't sure who she was talking to; herself or her husband, Henderson, who sat rocking back and forth in a chair on the front porch. Massie's chunky, white lace-up shoes sounded like repetitive hammering as she paced back and forth on the wooden planks.

After giving his wife ample time to process a very recent consideration, Henderson spoke. "I think it would be an answer to prayer," he said.

In May of 1929, Royce O'Reilly turned fifteen. He was born inside the walls of their large family home. One year later his sister, Merrigan came along. They, their friends and cousins, had "run loose" in Rockhill, Alabama. Their bare feet padded down red dirt roads and they relished ice cream on Sunday afternoons. Their faded overalls were torn by tree limbs that offered vantage points and stakeouts.

Royce's bright freckles and fire engine red hair made it impossible for him to blend in and go unnoticed. But, appearances aside, Royce O'Reilly's existence would not have allowed for anonominity.

The boy's electrically charged personality seemed to draw him toward the workings of wires. He wanted to get inside the very core of radios, amateur radio equipment and telephones. He learned Morse Code at age ten, and was making contacts around the world.

At age fourteen, Royce hooked up a radio to the household telephone, so that his sister's telephone conversations would be amplified throughout the house and onto the porch, for all passersby to hear.

Merrigan went crazy. She screamed unladylike expletives at her brother and went crying to her daddy.

The last thing Royce conducted before posing his request to attend military school, held an outcome that would weigh heavily in the direction of an affirmative answer from his parents.

The experiment, once again involved a telephone and electricity. But this time, the lives of townspeople outside of Royce's immediate family were at risk.

Royce went about his usual inventive business that summer day. His toolbox collection had grown and spilled over into apple crates and cloth drawstring bags. He didn't have a specific plan. Most of his creativity just evolved.

A twisted maze of resistors and capacitors lay inside the disassembled telephone. Royce saw an inviting screw terminal connection that begged to be hooked to wires left over from his last concoction. He worked diligently as if he were being relied upon to map out the inner workings of a national security system.

Lights dimmed, the radio crackled, and the telephone seemed to jump as one deafening ring jerked Royce into a rare tingle of fear.

Within fifteen minutes, "Big Pops Benefield," president of the local telephone company was banging on the door of the O'Reilly household. Big Pops yelled at the top of his lungs, "Royce O'Reilly, get the hell out here this minute before I come in there and kill you!" Royce's red head glowed through the black screen door as he looked up at the massive man. "Are you tryin' to electrocute all of my operators?! You damn near set 'th place on fire! My women are screamin' and coughin' from smoke. I think your daddy ought to put you on a one-way bus outta this town for good!"

Big Pops turned around and stomped his heavy feet back toward town.

"Yeah," Royce said to no one in particular. "Rockhill's getting a little boring." He thought about Georgia Military Academy. It was located in College Park, Georgia, which was very close to the big city of Atlanta. Royce imagined a spiffy new uniform and big city girls to admire him in it. There were girls' schools nearby and social activities on weekends. Rockhill High School just couldn't compete with what hopefully lay ahead in Georgia.

Henderson O' Reilly made a lasting impression on his son after the telephone company incident. The rest of the summer, Royce stuck to amateur radio and torturing his sister. Nothing too severe. He had already acquired his parents' permission to attend GMA, if his grades would allow his entrance into the elite establishment.

The letter came in July. Patrick Royce O'Reilly had been accepted to enter Georgia Military Academy as a freshman. The large packet filled with rules and regulations could wait. Royce wasn't too anxious to find out what all he "couldn't do."

Late August brought a nip of chill to the usually hot southern air. The morning coolness wrapped itself around Royce's bed and blew a wind of mixed emotions through his youthful mind. Alternating sadness and anticipation caused confusion. He would miss the friends he had been with since first grade. Royce wasn't all that sure why he wanted to go away to school, but it was too late to back out now.

Royce was startled out of his daydream state, when he saw Merrigan standing in the doorway.

"Hi, Pinky," she said.

"Oh, hi, Mer."

Royce sat up and propped against the headboard as Merrigan walked into his room. She positioned her slender frame at the foot of his bed and folded her legs to one side.

Even though she was his sister, Royce had to admit that Mer was the prettiest girl in town. Her chestnut wavy hair fell around her shoulders, and her green eyes sparkled when she talked. Merrigan was beautiful, popular and witty. He felt awkward and embarrassed as a lump was forming in his throat.

"I'll probably want to come home a lot on weekends," he said, refusing to meet her eyes.

"Ah, Pinky! You're gonna be going to those fancy balls. You'll have to fight the girls off with your BB gun!"

Royce gave her a playful shove and she dug her knuckles into his spiky red hair. They laughed, to cover up a painful time between siblings who cared deeply for each other.

"Hey Mer, will you come visit me at GMA sometime?"

"You bet I will, you brat. But I won't be coming to see you. I want to meet all those handsome boys in their uniforms!"

Merrigan flashed her best mischievous smile, ran down the stairs, and into the bathroom. There wasn't enough tissue to stifle her sobs and soak up her lonely tears.

Massie appeared nervous as she checked and re-checked Royce's supply list. Of course, the school would provide uniforms, but she was still afraid there was something she had overlooked. She had been up since dawn, cooking fried chicken. She made biscuits, and Royce's favorite chocolate cake. She wasn't an outwardly affectionate mother, but she wasn't going to let her boy go hungry on that long train ride.

Massie felt a sense of pride as she looked at her son. Royce had always been a handful, but her mother's intuition told her that he was going to be successful. Royce was going to make something out of himself and this was a step in the right direction.

Royce was dressed in a tweed suit, a crisp white shirt and brown tie. His shoes had been shined at the local barber shop and his red hair was slicked over to one side. He had put so much grease in his hair, that the red was toned down to a shiny auburn shade.

Royce kissed his mother, hugged Merrigan and joined his dad in the waiting car. Henderson drove down main street toward the railway station.

"Hey Dad, there's Phillips Morgan! And there's Carter Bynum with him. Reckon they know I'm leaving today?"

"Yep," replied Henderson. "I reckon the whole town knows about you, son."

The train ride was long. A lot of things ran through Royce's head during the hours that houses and telephone posts flew past him.

"Next stop, College Park!" The conductor's announcement came sooner than Royce was expecting. He must have fallen asleep. Royce grabbed the thick brown envelope, poured its contents into his lap and searched for the identification nametag he should have put on earlier. He found it and hastily pinned it to his lapel. "Royce O'Reilly—Freshman."

Uniformed young men filled the waiting platform. Royce had no idea that the train carried so many prospective GMA students. He thought the established students were waiting for him alone.

"Prickett, Stephenson, O'Reilly, this way! Hurry up, step it up! come on, you rats."

Royce's luggage was hoisted into a waiting bus with the words, Georgia Military Academy, painted on the sides. Last names were the rule, the regulation and the norm. His given name, "Royce," the one he had been so accustomed to hearing in negative and a few positive addresses, would vanish from his ears.

Young men were bumping into each other throughout the bus. "Excuse me, excuse me, please."

Royce finally found a vacant seat and was soon joined by a dark skinned boy The boy flashed a smile, held out his hand and introduced himself.

"I'm Kelley Watkins from Chattanooga." Royce reciprocated with an introduction and handshake. Royce felt self-conscious as he looked at the handsome boy with a good tan. He was suddenly aware of his freckles and fair skin that didn't take to the sun.

Everything was so new. Royce felt a jolt in his stomach like he had never experienced. It was fear, excitement and homesickness all combined. He had no idea what to expect. But he looked around at the other boys on the bus and imagined they were having similar emotions.

The bus drove around curves and up hills, until a large impressive looking arena of buildings came into view. The leaves were just beginning to turn and float off of the trees. Royce felt like the leaves. Floating and not knowing where he would land.

Several buses lined up in front of a quadrangle with a large building in the center. Boys bumped and crowded each other as they impatiently headed down the steps and scattered into the fresh air.

Signs were everywhere. Arrows pointing the way to registration for classes, room assignments and uniform distribution. Upperclassmen were asserting their higher authority and inundating the freshmen with their "exceptional knowledge" of the school they had become so familiar with. They pointed and pushed the younger boys in so many directions that Royce's head was spinning. The freshmen were called, "Rats, Baby faces, Mama's boys," "Dumb bells" and more.

Royce was escorted to the room that would be home for nine months. He dropped his belongings on a neatly made bed. Starched white pillow cases and sheets which where folded back slightly over a gray wool blanket. Royce quickly moved his luggage to the floor. He lamented the suspicion that it would be his responsibility to keep the bed covers crisp and tucked every single day. And that was only a hint of the discipline to come.

Just as Royce was taking a deep breath and blowing out regrets, his roommate entered. Amazing! thought Royce. It was Kelley Watkins, the tanned boy he had met on the bus. Seeing that familiar face made Royce feel a little less alone.

Royce and Kelley shook hands for the second time and faced the rest of the day together.

Students were lined up to receive wool pants, kaki shirts and a dark blue tie. Webbed belts with brass buckles that were expected to shine like the sun every single day. Caps for daily wear and caps for formal wear. A full military uniform with elaborate cord designs on the sleeves and across the front. At the end of each looped design was a brass button. The same cord designs sat royally on a collar so high that Royce knew he would be choked to death. Wide white straps made an "X" across the chest and held a huge diamond shaped piece of brass right in the middle. A wide white belt accompanied the uniform with yet, another large brass buckle. The pants were fairly simple, thank goodness, thought Royce.

All of that brass to polish, all of the studying to do. When and where did the fun come in? A sinking feeling covered Royce's spirit as he carried the heavy uniforms to his dorm room. But then, a picture came into his mind. A picture he saw in the information book. Young men in their formal uniforms dancing with beautiful girls dressed in evening gowns. Maybe he could invite his hometown love, Albertine King.

A day in the life of the students began at six o'clock with breakfast served in a large mess hall. By seven

forty-five there was morning formation where atten-
dance was checked, the United States flag raised, and
uniform inspection conducted. The students then proceeded to their respective classes. After seven periods
with a lunch break, Royce was struggling to stay awake.
It would take weeks before he became accustomed to
such a tight schedule.

Royce enjoyed Social Studies, Spanish, English
and other required subjects. He liked his teachers and
enjoyed their individual eccentric personalities. Physical Education was not his favorite activity, but he
endured it.

An announcement was made during P.E. that for
those who decided to go out for track, there would be a
cake race. The idea of winning a cake took over all
thought of the exertion and exhaustion of running. Royce
signed up.

He nearly died trying to win that cake. He didn't
even come close to winning, and he was stuck being on
the track team. His track leader was also his history
teacher. History was Royce's weakest subject. He knew
he would be terrible at track and he could just see a big
"F" in history due to his lack of athletic ability. Royce
had confidence in his inventive mind to come up with
something.

One night after supper, Royce went to his room
and sat down at his desk. He placed a clean piece of
typing paper in the black Underwood and set his mind
to reeling.

October 5, 1929
Dear Drudder,

I am very alarmed to hear that you are going out for track. I told you that you should watch your heart condition that you have had since childhood. You must tell your coach that I said you need to be dismissed from this strenuous activity. Your mother and I are seriously concerned about you. Take care of this situation as soon as you receive my letter.

Love,

Daddy

Royce neatly folded the deceptive letter and waited for the morning.

Royce sat through history class with a funny feeling in the pit of his stomach. He waited for the bell and for the classroom to empty itself of identically dressed students. He approached the desk of his coach/teacher and handed him the letter. He watched as Major Spivey read. He looked up at the somewhat soft, red-headed boy and said, "O'Reilly, Because this is such a serious matter, I am going to excuse you from the track team. Take care of yourself, boy, alright?"

Royce thanked his teacher and walked out of the room. He could have sworn he saw a twinkle in Major Spivey's eye.

Overall, Royce's grades were pretty good. Much better than they would have been in his hometown school, but he had been dealing with love sickness over Albertine King. By November, it had grown worse. Royce felt confident that he would be granted a pass to go home.

O'Reilly! the commanding officer blurted out. Of course you can't leave this weekend! Aren't you aware that we are having government inspection?!

Royce was going to have to be inventive once again. In his fifteen year-old mind, he could not wait until the next weekend. He had to see Albertine as soon as possible.

Albertine attended a Catholic girls school in Alabama, but Royce knew that she came home every weekend.

Royce and his roommate, Kelley had become very good friends. They confided in each other and Royce knew that Kelley would never tell.

The alarm clock was set for 3:00 a.m. Royce dressed, packed a few things and sneaked out of the academy. He caught a street car and went as far as it would go toward his home town. He got off and started hitch hiking. He was picked up enough times to get him as far Birmingham, which was fifty miles from Rockhill.

Royce's parents were not to pleasantly surprised to hear that their boy was at a hotel in Birmingham, Alabama. They got in their car and drove the fifty miles. "That boy, that boy" was all they could say.

They made it back to Rockhill around dusk. Royce quickly spoke to his sister and then took off for the house around the corner.

"Mrs. King, could I see Albertine, please?" I'm sorry, Royce. Albertine stayed at school this weekend. Mrs. King could see Royce's face turn white which made his freckles more prominent. She thought he was going to be sick. "Thank you, Mam. I'll try again sometime."

Saturday night, Royce slept deep and long in his bed at home. At ten o' clock, his mother woke him for church. "You'd better get up and go to church," Massie said in her authoritative voice. You've got some serious praying to do.

Reality hit Royce over bacon and eggs. He could hardly swallow due to the fearful lump that had formed in his throat and went all the way to his stomach.

Leaving school in the wee hours of the morning seemed exciting. And his love for Albertine drove him into another place in his mind. A place that went no farther than the moment. Now he would have to face the music and officers and no telling what kind of punishment.

Henderson and Massie drove Royce all the way to Atlanta. Nothing much was said among the three of them. Royce's thoughts were racing. there just wasn't a course in "staying out of trouble." And even if there was, he would flunk it anyway.

Monday morning deliberation would come soon. The full commander who resided on Royce's floor knocked on the door of room number 219. "Royce O'Reilly?" "Yes sir." "You are to be at the main office of this academy at one o'clock sharp. Do you understand?" "Yes sir."

Breakfast was no good and his mind did not attend classes. His heart pounded and he thought maybe he really was having heart trouble. "I shouldn't have faked that letter," Royce thought to himself. I'm going to die right here and now! But, then again, that might be better than having to face the commanding officers.

The efficient secretary called Royce's name and opened a large elaborately carved door. The office was plush and in contrast to the men who sat upright in a circle of straight backed chairs. Royce's eyes went directly to the person he had hoped would not be there. The founder and president of Georgia Military Academy, Colonel John Charles Woodward.

Royce knew he was done for. He was dead meat. It was over. It was back to Rockhill and bad grades.

"O'Reilly!" Colonel Woodward spoke first. "What made you think you could leave this campus when, number one, you were denied a pass, and number two, this academy was preparing for an exceedingly important time of federal inspection?!" "I don't know, sir." Royce's voice cracked as he looked down at the floor.

"Step out of the room O' Reilly while we discuss your retribution." "Yes sir."

Royce's sentence was to carry his rifle and pack while walking forty hours around the bull ring. His steps became a cadence and the sweat dripping from his forehead, heralded a rhythm to Albertine. "Albertine King, Albertine King, Albertine King. And even though he didn't get to see her, she was worth it.

Seasons came and went and Royce's troublemaking tapered off. The good education that he acquired at GMA enabled him to be accepted at the University of Alabama.

Royce joined a fraternity at the university. The life there was nothing like military school. Things weren't as structured. But that was alright. He was ready for a break.

Merrigan was a sophomore at the university. She and Royce planned a weekend home to Rockhill. But Royce's sister waited until the last minute to tell him that she was bringing a friend. She drove up to the Pi Kappa Phi house and found Royce waiting with his suitcase.

"Hi, Pinky!" Merrigan said enthusiastically. "I wish she would quit calling me that," thought Royce. "Especially in front of other people." "Hey, Pinky, I want you to meet Alice Lee Goodwin from Montgomery. Alice Lee, this is my brother, Royce." Royce looked at the girl beside his sister and could not believe that such a vision was going to spend the weekend at his house. "Alice Lee is a freshman like you and I thought y'all might like to talk university life."

Royce climbed in the back seat and was silent. He was as quiet as he was the day his parents drove him back to GMA. "Albertine King" he thought. I wonder what ever happened to her.

One thing Royce could say about his mother, was that she really knew how to do things up right. The house was shiny and fresh sheets were on the beds. Delicious meals were served on fine china with the family gathered around the large dining room table. Although his mother was a good cook, it wasn't her favorite activity. That's where Nelly came in. She had been with the family since Royce's earliest memory.

Nelly was old now. Dark as the inside of a cave and sweet as a flower. She was quite a cook. Alice Lee was impressed with the entire O'Reilly family and their hospitality. The feeling was mutual. Massie and Henderson were very taken with Alice Lee.

Royce never thought of himself as good-looking, although at age eighteen, he was coming into his own and looking quite handsome. He was oblivious to that fact.

Alice Lee was easy to talk to. She was a little shy, but that was alright. Royce would have been happy just to stare at her blue eyes, blonde hair, and slender figure.

But, Alice Lee was Merrigan's friend and they spent a lot of time talking and acting silly.

Saturday night, Merrigan, Alice Lee and Royce went to see the THREE STOOGES at the Neeley picture show. They loaded up on popcorn and coke. Royce laughed with the movie crowd, but mostly he was thinking about Alice Lee.

After three years at the University of Alabama, Royce was becoming bored to death. "What was the point?" He had a job waiting for him at home, working in his dad's business. After a year at the university, Alice Lee transferred to Birmingham Southern College. Merrigan had already graduated and was planning to be married.

So, Royce packed up and left. College just wasn't for him. He worked with his dad and dated Lena Charlton. He thought it was the real thing. Lena seemed quite a catch. But the war was stirring and Royce was drafted. He said goodbye to Lena and thought his world had ended.

Lena and Royce wrote letters, but eventually their love faded. Royce began to remember Alice Lee. He got her address from Merrigan and wrote her a letter. He was excited when she wrote back and told him she was single.

Royce's engagement to Alice Lee was just too exciting for words. They spent a lot of time talking and learning about their respective pasts. Royce told Alice Lee about having attended GMA. "You're kidding me, Royce!" Alice Lee shreeked. "My aunt Laurie's brother is the founder and president of that school! What a coincedence! We just MUST invite him to the wedding. Can't you just imagine how thrilled he would be to see you?"

Royce 's entire life at military school flashed before his very eyes. His face felt hot and he was a little sick to his stomach. But it was too late. He was in love with Alice Lee. He would tactfully suggest a very intimate ceremony.

INDEPENDENT LIVING

Martha Louise Wakefield entered the large automatic doors of her independent living facility. A colorful scarf was tied around her head and she clutched the knot tightly. She was outside for only a minute, but she, and her generation believed full-well, that one square of cloth, folded in a triangle, would ward off colds and other infirmities.

She exited the car that her son-in-law parked by the door, and held her daughter's arm. A week of vacationing with her family in Palm Beach had ended and she was glad for the freedom she felt inside her community's walls.

Palm Beach was too big. The little individual cottages that the family rented were confusing. The steps from her cottage to another's were too great a task to undertake.

Martha Louise wanted to get back to her four rooms and regular meals in a dining room where she recognized faces. She didn't want any more strange food with uncommon sauces. Wine made her dizzy, but she drank it to be sociable. She didn't want anymore of that. At least, not until next year. She might go next year, if she was still around, which, according to Martha Louise, she probably wouldn't be.

A couple of old ladies were seated in wicker chairs and absorbing sunshine on the veranda. "Hey, Hattie.

Did ya miss me?" "Where did you go?" Martha, in her gravely southern drawl, made sure that Hattie and others who still had their hearing, knew she had been absent. "I've been gone uh week with th children an grandchildren. We had uh wonda-ful time." "Well, I'll say," replied Hattie, a former school teacher who was petite and attractive. Hattie was sharp, even though she didn't know Anne had been gone.

The conversation on the sun-drenched porch was short and to the point. Martha Louise asked if anything had happened while she was away. Somebody died. Several of the women tossed around the question of who it might have been. One woman heard nothing and continued her knitting.

"Who died this week, Velma?" "Oh, I believe it was that Forrest woman.

She refused to take anymore medicine." Well, that's too bad," was Martha's response as she shuffled toward the entrance hall of her recent home.

People in their eighties don't pay much attention to death unless it's a family member or close friend.

Jim and Martha Louise Wakefield, began traveling extensively soon after their only child entered college. They saw the world and each time they returned, Martha made the same comment. "I bleeve ma travlin' days ah ovah." Six months later, Jim was cooking up another trip, and Martha Louise gladly went along.

This yearly vacation had been nothing like the others before. When Jim was alive, he'd gather up the family to escape winter. Long treks to warm climates. Palm trees, cruises and tropical breezes for everyone.

Martha's husband of sixty years, eternally youthful, stood on the decks of ships in white pants, sweater, and signature hat. He took brisk morning walks while Martha sat inside. He was six years her senior, yet he took care of everything. He took care of too much. She held onto his arm and she held onto his abilities. She was nothing without him, or so she thought.

Martha Louise rode the elevator to her apartment on the second floor. She slowly walked behind her daughter, who held her carry-on bag. Her body was light and frail and her feet barely made an imprint in the thick carpet. She passed seating areas, furnished in elegant style, swathed in lush fabrics and accessorized to perfection. She walked down familiar halls; galleries for appropriate and tastefully framed paintings.

Martha struggled with her purse and finally pulled out the key that would give her a sense of relief. The key to her mother's antiques, and acquisitions shared with Jim.

Martha cried like a baby in the shower. It was impossible to tell where the warm water began and her hot tears ended. She screamed and cursed while white foamy soap ran down the drain.

She dressed, wrapped herself in layers and sat on her deck overlooking scenic mountains. She shed more tears of longing for the love of her life. Martha sipped her coffee and ached for her husband's guiding hand. "This indupendunt livin is foe th burds," she said to no one. "If I had gone first, Jim would jus go on with his life. He would have uh ball an nevah look back!"

Martha had tried to stay on in the home she shared with Jim, but living alone was not something she wanted to tackle. She couldn't open the top to her cranberry juice. Jim had always had strong hands. She was in constant fear of falling. Jim, at eighty six, could roll her in a wheelchair, on an incline at the airport. She could still drive, but not well and not far. Jim drove any and everywhere he wanted to go.

She had no hobbies. She had given up playing Bridge years before. She was even losing interest in crossword puzzles. She belonged to the "Gab Club," but they only met once a month for socializing and lunch. The club was a spin-off of Bridge clubs from the 1950s. Several of the women were still living and new ones had been inducted.

The Gab Club girls dressed up and met at a country club fifty miles away. The youngest member, who was around seventy three, packed her van with old ladies and drove on the highways like a maniac. It seemed a dangerous occupation for someone like Martha Louise, who was afraid of everything. But she didn't notice dodging cars and near misses. She sat in her seat and participated in simultaneous talking.

Martha and her only daughter, Sandra, had tolerated each other since the day Sandra emerged from the womb fifty-eight years before. At times, the toleration became intolerable. Sandra was a daddy's girl and her grief lay heavier than anything she had experienced. She had lost her hero and been left to care for a parent she'd never gotten to know.

But Sandra made a promise to herself to keep the peace. To do things for her mother and to accept the responsibility with strength. That's what her daddy would have done. He always told her it was "that universal mother-daughter thing" and that was the reason they didn't "gee-haw." But Sandra took it personally and felt guilty most of the time.

Nothing was said between Sandra and her mother, after Jim's death. The fighting just stopped. The clashes and criticisms evaporated. Where did they go? Sandra didn't really care about the question or the answer. She just accepted the truce, wherever it came from.

"The home" was not what the reference implied. It was known as Essex Place and housed the elderly who were, "privileged," so to speak. Mostly women whose husbands had provided well for them.

There were a few widowed men and a number of couples. Some of the married ones who lost spouses, married again, right there at Essex Place. It was embarrassing to Martha Louise to think about those old women chasing men.

But most of the women weren't interested in establishing romantic relationships. They joked and laughed, played bridge and danced to daily musical entertainment. Some of them used walkers, all had lost loved ones. Some couldn't hear and some went in and out of reality.

Martha watched in amazement. She saw joy and humor come out of old age and sorrow. She saw strength and fortitude in women who had no one to lean on.

The women of Essex Place were fashion conscious and Martha picked up on their couture. If one had something, the others had to have it too. She noticed the shoes first. A certain style that sent women residents in droves to shoe stores all over town. They took their walkers, and their oxygen. They hobbled up the steps of Essex Place buses.

They scouted out summer white flats with rubber soles and enough straps to keep the shoes from slipping off. When autumn arrived, the run was on for black. Martha acquired a collection of white, black, tan and red shoes, all in the same sensible style.

In time, Martha Louise Wakefield forgot that it "wasn't proper" to laugh loudly at funny things people said. She appeared to have forgotten most of the "disrespectful" things that Sandra had done to make her life so miserable.

In her immense grief and loss, she was unfolding and displaying the personality of an appealing little old lady. For the first time in her life, Sandra was drawn to her mother's persona.

Sandra was surprised at the steps her mother was taking. She thought she saw a hint of courage and a determination to make the best of things. Martha began taking Bridge lessons. The game of her youth was coming back to her and her mind was active again.

She made crafts, which in the past had seemed a "silly activity for a grown woman." She laughed at herself, her mistakes and antics. She made friends, popped popcorn in the microwave and invited them over. She read large print books and exchanged them with fellow readers. She picked up "senior citizen buzz words and lingo."

Martha Louise joined The Red Hat Club. Twenty to fifty elderly women decked out in purple dresses and red hats for luncheon outings. Martha, who had been so self conscious and concerned with "what will people think?" was wearing a red hat and purple dress in public.

Who was this woman? questioned Sandra. Who on earth was coming out from underneath such a rigid southern belle?

When Sandra's daddy died, there was no unfinished business hanging for either of them. They had said everything to each other. They were tight and there were no loose ends. No guilt, no regrets.

If Sandra's mother had gone first, she would never have known. Never known what it could have been like to develop a relationship and break the cycle of mother-daughter controversy. She would have assumed that it wasn't to be. An impossible bond with an unlikely person. And Sandra would have grieved out of disappointment and remorse.

Sandra sat by the phone and gazed out at barren winter trees. She and her husband lived within thirty minutes of Essex Place. It was almost time for her 10:00 a.m. call to her mother. A daily ritual. The conversations were lasting longer and feeling easier. Martha would tell Sandra that she had been to "sittersize" and was "woe-un out." She'd relate what she ate for breakfast and who called the night before. She'd tell about the latest book she was reading, and then mention the dream she'd had about Jim. Plans would be made for weekly lunch and shopping.

Sandra's thoughts drifted back to a day on the beach when she was fifteen and her mother, a beautiful forty. Something her mother said made her laugh that day.

They giggled together like schoolgirls, there on the expanse of sand where cars drove back and forth. A forgotten memory. A pleasant time, and a glimpse into Martha Louise.

THE PARTY

Summer in our small southern town is the best time in the world! I am eight years old and it is a Wednesday in 1952.

Today, Mama doesn't plan to leave me in the care of my grandmother next door. This Wednesday, the Bridge club will meet at our house because it's Mama's turn to entertain.

Preparations begin in the morning and move slowly in the July heat. Mama stirs up a dessert which I long for. I have never seen anyone scrape every smidgen of creamy mixture out of a bowl like my mama can. Very little left to lick.

I watch as card tables are set up. Crisp starched linens, silver and crystal transform the brown, well worn tables into banquet fare. Our little house sparkles and I know by heart, delicious smells that will mingle together and remain long after the party is over.

On Bridge Club day, Daddy eats at the Gold Star Restaurant. On regular days, he comes home from the office at 12:00 noon. Dinner in the middle of a good playing day is such a waste of time. Mama calls me in from my sand box or riding my bike. The three of us sit at the kitchen table and there it is, another big plate of food for me to try and consume.

When I grow up, I am going to have a sandwich and call it "lunch" like they do in New York City. Their night meal is called, "dinner" and it's really fancy. They do all kinds of wonderful things in New York City because I see them on the television. They don't even talk like we do.

Once when I was watching Howdy Doody, Buffalo Bob told all of us to be sure and wash our hands and faces before dinner. I went into the bathroom before suppertime, (which is called, "dinner" where Buffalo Bob lives) and began splashing water on my face. Mama saw me and started screaming, "What on earth are you doing?!" I told her, and she said for me to march myself right out of there and never do that again. It was ok to wash my hands before supper, but washing my face would surely cause me to get Pneumonia. I wondered about all of the kids in New York and if they had gotten Pneumonia from washing their faces before dinnertime.

The Bridge club ladies arrive and I listen to the sounds they make. I enjoy certain sounds. When I go to the picture show downtown, I like to hear the actors and actresses walk on the sidewalks, and tap dance. When a lot of people tap dance at the same time, it sounds great. It makes me want to go home, put on my tap shoes and dance all over the house. But I never sound as good to myself as they do in the movies.

Dressed up ladies wear fashionable clothes that rustle. I tune my ears to their high heels on the waxed wooden floors. Spoons tinkle as coffee is stirred and forks clink against good china. The women taste "the best dessert they have ever put in their mouths." I wonder if they brag on everybody's dessert like that, no matter who has the Bridge Club.

After dessert and coffee, the tables are stripped of their glamour and the serious game of Bridge begins. A sudden quiet lingers as the cards are shuffled, dealt, picked up and fanned out. Bright red fingernails click on brown tables, and the women ponder clubs, diamonds, spades, and hearts in their hands. The silence is dotted with utterances of "hummm."

Then, like a boom of thunder out of a quiet rain, the boisterous laughter begins. Their voices rise and fall like a roller coaster. The laughter turns to sporadic giggles, and giggles into whispers of gossip. The cycle repeats itself.

I am disgusted and burning with curiosity at the same time. I don't want to grow up and act like they do. It's embarrassing. I meander back to my room or out into the yard. I want to leave, yet I want to hide behind a door to smell the coffee, perfume and cigarettes. Try to decipher the language of that secret society.

There were a number of Bridge clubs in town during the forties, and fifties. There was time then, for friends to get together in a relaxed atmosphere. Kids weren't involved in sports, except for the high school boys who played football in the fall.

I assumed I would grow up and imitate the customs familiar to my mother. Thought I would eventually be a Bridge club lady. But something deep inside of me dreaded the time when I might have to learn the game and sit still. It seemed so complicated and important.

Time would show me that on the different road I was to take, I could indeed survive without learning the game of Bridge. I tried it in college, but the sorority girls made fun of me. I was too "artsy" and lacking in mathmatical skills to keep up with "who had played what."

As the members of this institution grew older, there was less Bridge and more talk. They discovered country clubs in the nearby city, and began getting together for luncheons. Bridge faded, children grew up and parents took off to see the world. They traveled to Europe, went on cruises and enjoyed their empty nests.

Friends have passed away and new friends have moved into town. There will always be a ladies' club. Now, the coffee is a little weaker and smoking has been given up. The game of Bridge is left to the younger generation.

But on occasions when I am invited to join this lively group, I become a kid again. It is still 1950 and I am excited and intrigued. Billie, Darlene, Mary Frances and Mama are young and beautiful, and the party will never end.

THE POINT

What was the point? The point was, that I didn't shed bitterness and self absorption until I grew old enough to wish I had done it long before.

They rounded the curve in their old people's car. All the years of moving, being uprooted. All those different houses with their driveways that led to a daughter's uncertain greeting. They rounded the curves to see about my boys and me.

Anything that was broken, he fixed. She brought food because she sensed we needed it. They were moral and upstanding. I had allowed myself to be pounded like a wooden stake. Thrust into a personal hell that I shared with no one. "It was their fault" I concluded. It had to be. Why couldn't they fix me? Why couldn't they give me enough money to fix me?

They rounded the curve in their old people's car the other day. Were they certain of the warm welcome that awaited them or was there still caution in their souls? I pray for the former.

The sun was shining like a neon light that spring day. The breeze stroked my body and told me I was forgiven. We ate at the cafeteria and everything was good. I'm her "personal shopper" now. She's not able to unbutton, zip and glide into and out of stiff new clothes. I see her eighty year old bones and remember the glamorous photo of a girl at the beach. Looks don't

mean anything. She is beautiful to me now in her frail-
ness.

Daddy is eighty five. Spry, sharp and charming.
The temporal nature of him hits me in the heart and
reflects back from his blue eyes. His eyes are the only
indication that he knows his time on this earth is limited. But there is resolution, forgiveness and intense
love among the three of us.

Let me serve now. I'll round the curves and fix the
broken things.

THE TWO GRANDMOTHERS

Effie disappeared. For a whole day. Elizabeth, her oldest granddaughter walked down the building's corridors, as she had done many times before. Nothing out of the ordinary for a teenage girl. She had something to drop off at her Grandma's.

The beautiful independent living facility was occupied by people Effie's age. Essex Place was a home for "comfortable" old people to spend their latter years, being waited on and looked after. It would not have been easy to just slip out.

Effie was popular among the geriatric group, and younger people, as well. Her grandchildren adored her. Her no-nonsense spirit and feisty wit drew people in. She was the one who could get things done when others were too shy to ask.

Effie seemed to be in her right mind most of the time. She couldn't hear well, and sometimes the affliction made people think she wasn't at herself. She had the physical limitation of having to carry oxygen around with her all of the time. She couldn't have just left. Not without the assistance of someone to help her into a car, or a cab or bus. Effie had such a presence, that her absence was noticed by those who didn't notice much of anything.

Elizabeth went directly to her grandmother's room. She expected to walk in with her goods and find her grandma, among books, pictures and antiques. Effie wasn't much for decorating, but the things she owned created an elegant, yet lived in appearance.

The apartment was a miniature of the house she occupied for forty years with her late husband, Johnny. They raised three children, Effie cooked mounds of delicious food and hosted frequent Bridge parties. The house had an inviting chaotic, pack-rat, rich southern ambiance. Her apartment was a pared-down re-creation of the same.

Elizabeth knocked and waited for her hearing-impaired grandmother to come to the door. Nothing. Enough time had passed to muster panic in the young girl.

Alice and Effie shared the privilege of being grandmothers to the offspring of their respective divorced children. Their union produced two boys who were the finest on God's green earth. That connection created a bond between the two women.

Elizabeth considered Alice a part of the family. The feeling was mutual. Alice loved Effie's family and enjoyed being around them. So, it was natural for Elizabeth to begin her search by knocking on Alice's door.

Elizabeth was crying at that point. "I can't find Grandma!" She's just gone. She didn't tell anybody she was leaving. I don't know what to do!"

Effie and Alice were total opposites, from their body language to the level of their voices. Effie didn't "ask" people to do things for her, she "told" them. She used to be tall and a fast walker. Even in her last years, she held herself up straight and looked attractive with her thick white hair. She would have been called "a handsome woman" in the south.

Alice was becoming more petite every year. She was delicate, shy and reserved. She was a beauty in her younger days. Glamorous pictures of Alice, filled age-worn pages of Birmingham Southern College's yearbooks from the 1930s.

The "beauty" turned into a "cute" little old lady. Alice had all of her original teeth. Really good teeth. She learned to open her mouth and flash a beautiful smile that she had hidden for decades.

Thanks to bleaching strips and a looser attitude, she just let that smile go. Alice had never been witty, although I think it's possible that she took "sense of humor classes" at Essex Place. She learned to laugh at herself occasionally. Maybe it was Effie's influence.

On the day of Effie's disappearance, Elizabeth's distress, and a genuine concern for her friend, prompted Alice to get busy. She looked everywhere. In her slow shuffle, she walked the halls and knocked on doors. She made phone calls to Effie's children and checked with the front desk. She contacted friends in the complex, but no one knew anything about where she might have gone.

Alice convinced management to unlock Effie's apartment. She was not lying on the floor, playing out everyone's worst fears. The morning turned into afternoon and still, no Effie.

Effie showed up at the front door in time for dinner's early seating. She rolled her oxygen cart across the foyer and held her attractive gray head high. She was greeted by hysterical women who wanted to know where on earth she had been. "Why?" this and "why?" that and "we were so worried!"

"I went to play Bridge at Mary McClearin's house," Mahan replied in her matter-of-fact, very southern voice.

She could not understand why everyone was so worked up.

Things were always happening at Essex Place. Just when boredom was setting in, something would occur to give the residents a lot to talk about.

Alice knew better than to try and cut her own toenails. She couldn't see, she couldn't bend over and she had a podiatrist. I suppose things were dull at Essex Place that night. She probably wanted a break from reading her large print book. Or, she didn't want to wait for the doctor, who clipped them with ease and professionalism.

Alice bent over as far as she could, holding a pair of surgically sharp nail scissors. Her bifocals misrepresented the position of her feet, and she took the end of her toe off in one clean whack.

The phrase, "bled like a stuck pig," did not even begin to describe the red liquid that poured out of Alice's toe. She did not call 911, or even the desk at Essex. She called Effie, Effie who got things done.

Effie grabbed her oxygen cart, bag, tubes, paraphernalia, and took the elevator one flight up to Alice's room. Along the way, she knocked on doors and called out to women who were gathered in the halls. Effie was the Pied Piper, leading women with walkers and canes.

Metal banged into walls, against feet and thumped onto carpet. Blind leading the blind, oxygen tanks, and curiosity seekers who went along for some excitement. At least fifteen women entered Alice's apartment and gazed upon blood-soaked towels. Effie called 911.

Paramedics and a nurse rushed over to room 220. The foot was bandaged and instructions given to make an appointment with the Podiatrist first thing the next morning. Everyone exited Alice's room more slowly than they entered and things settled down for the night. For that night, anyway.

Being hooked up to oxygen was a hindrance to someone like Effie. She was a woman on the go. She had worked in an office, driven whenever and wherever she wanted and lead an all around active life. But in spite of her obstacles, she managed to keep her spirits up and make the best of the situation.

Although Effie couldn't hear very well, she heard the sound of her oxygen tank making an annoying buzz. She put up with it for a couple of days. But by midnight of the second night, she had had enough!

In the middle of the night, Effie called the oxygen maintenance man and was not in the least bit concerned that he might be asleep. "Get over here right now! My oxygen tank has been making a noise for two days and I can't stand it any longer!"

"Yes Mam, Mrs. Harris, I'll be right over."

Mr. Mays, the oxygen repair man, must have been a saint. He entered Effie's apartment and thoroughly examined the tank, tubes and valves. No noise was coming from the oxygen supply.

The only noise Mr. Mays heard, was the buzzer on Effie's alarm clock. Mr. Mays turned off the alarm clock beside Effie's bed. He delicately told his elderly customer that it probably was an accident, or that the housekeeper did it. He gathered up his things and hoped that he could get back to sleep before morning called him again.

Alice and Effie were expecting their first great-grandchild. Alice had only one child, a daughter. Her two sons were Alice's only grandchildren. Effie had three children and six grandchildren. A big family to dote on her. She thought it was very nice that she would become a great-grandmother, but Alice was ecstatic.

Sonograms, or whatever they're called nowadays, are much improved from earlier years when all one could see was a fuzzy blob of motion. They are so clear, in fact that features are detectable and the sex of the child determined.

Alice was overjoyed to see the black and white pictures which showed a perfect facial profile of the little girl who would be a part of herself and the other great-grandmother.

After commenting on the adorable little upturned nose, her first question to Effie was drawled out in her crackly southern accent. "What culah is th hair?" Technology is good, but it has it's limitations.

There was life outside of Essex Place. Fortunately Effie and Alice were among those who were able to socialize beyond the walls of independent living. The entertainment committee provided for Bridge parties, shopping, lunches, teas and church activities.

Effie lived most of her life in Huntsville, Alabama and knew many people in the community. She moved to Essex a year or two before Alice and therefore knew the ropes. She stayed in close contact with her "in town" friends and included Alice in her group.

The United Methodist Women hold what is known as, "circle meetings." They get together for study, eating and talking.

Effie's circle planned a Christmas party and Alice was invited. Christmas sweaters were a must among the senior citizen crowd, and that was a day for everyone to show off their finest.

A longtime friend of Effie's, became her personal shopper. Shopping was not easy for Effie, due to being hooked up to oxygen twenty four hours a day. The friend knew Effie's style, and brought beautiful clothes to add to her wardrobe. She brought a colorful new Christmas sweater for Effie to wear to the church luncheon.

Their ride came and Alice sat next to Effie in the backseat. Alice was not terribly observant, but she did wonder why Effie's Christmas sweater looked so dull. She wondered if her eyes were getting worse. There was no design on the sweater except for a few random strings hanging here and there.

Someone else noticed the unusual pattern, so Alice was reassured that she wasn't losing her mind. Effie Harrison had dressed that morning and put her new sweater on inside out and backwards. While riding in the car, and with the help of her companions, Effie pulled tubes out of her nose, took the sweater off, turned it right-side-out, reattached her oxygen and walked into the church without a hitch.

After two hours, on a dark winter afternoon, Alice had reached her highest level of anxiety. She sat in Effie's apartment and rubbed her eyes underneath her glasses. She rubbed her eyes and gritted her teeth. The "teeth-gritting thing" looked like a combination of a quick smile and a grimace. The movements became more frequent with Alice's growing anticipation. Rubbing and gritting.

Sometimes her daughter had to physically remove herself from those annoying repetitive motions. But she wasn't there that day. As far as Alice was concerned, her daughter could have gone to another planet with her husband, children and everyone she held dear. She was "cut off from the outside world" and Effie was her only anchor.

It all started when Alice picked up her telephone to make a casual call to her only daughter. There was no tone. The phone was dead! Alice's shuffle reached record pace when she crossed the hall and breathlessly knocked on her neighbor's door.

"Is your phone dead, May-ree Clay-ah?"

Mary Claire's telephone was not dead, nor was anyone else's on the second floor. Alice went to Effie's apartment. She was able to call her daughter's number because Mahan had it written down. Alice did not know anyone's number. They were programmed into her telephone so that all she had to do was punch a button. Alice's only child had "no business" being at the grocery store or anywhere else, but that's where she was.

She returned home from shopping to hear not one, but two hysterical, messages on the answer machine.

"Lucy!!! Call me! Call me as soon as you get home! I don't know Tom's sale phone numbah an I kant get in touch with any body. My phone is day-ed, day-ed an I'm gettin panicky."

Second message: "Lucy!!! Call me up at Effie's apahhtment. Oh, Effie, no tellin when she'll get home. No tellin! Tom's probly awreddy left work an on his way home an I don't know his sale phone numbah! Lucy!!! call me as soon as ya get this message!

I guess this was one area where Effie just didn't have the answer. They had tried to call maintenance, but maintenance couldn't help with that problem. They didn't think about calling the telephone company.

In utter distress and feeling like no one was meeting her immediate needs, Alice went back to her apartment. She searched through drawers and finally found a book with a list of telephone numbers. There was Tom's cell phone number! She went back over to Mary Claire's. Alice was the only person in all of Essex Place whose world was completely cut off.

Lucy's husband, Tom, is the calmest man on the face of the earth. He is patient, flexible and filled with compassion.

"Alice, have you checked to see if one of you telephones might be off of the hook?" Tom asked.

"Why, no." replied Alice. The thought had never occurred to her. The receiver on one of her telephones was indeed, tilted off of the hook. She supposed the maid did it.

RIGHTS OF PASSAGE

Oliver had been with me for 27 years. I know that life without him would have been easier. But this addition to my heart has helped me learn things about life, I suppose. That's the way it works, isn't it? We learn from the hard times.

Often, I think I would rather have been ignorant of his status, his existence. Sometimes Ollie drove me crazy with his annoying way of popping in at will. He disturbed my routine, yet his nature was always forgiving of this sporadic, unpredictable mother.

I remember when the boys were young. I saw Oliver follow along behind them during their escapades. He wove in and out of the two when they ran on the beach. He was in front, in the middle and behind them. At times, he seemed to disappear, become the same clear blue as the ocean. He would just vanish. And then, appear inside the soft foam of breaking waves.

The boys didn't get to know Ollie. There was no opportunity. They had each other and they were tight. As far as they knew, he wasn't there.

I felt so terribly sad in that deep mother crevice that is sometimes a distant, dull pain, other times, a stabbing knife.

Ollie left me for long periods of time. And when he did, I pretended he didn't exist. He could stay away for months and then show up at a festive gathering. He ruined my good time. I felt guilty and furious until the wine warmed me and temporarily took away the hurt.

When Jack and Stan went off to college, I was left with Ollie. His presence became more constant and predictable. I missed his brothers but if I was honest with myself, I didn't want another child interfering with my life. I didn't want to have to deal with who he was, what he was. It was time for the empty nest. He was as big as life itself and would not leave.

I was getting older but Ollie still seemed so young. Like he hadn't had a chance to be what he should have been. I did not know what to do with him and I didn't know what to do with myself, where he was concerned.

I decided to drive to the coast. Six hours with Ollie beside me. The history I had with him grew like a poisonous vine. The vine was binding and choking me. I couldn't break free. Most of the drive was in silence except for my intermittent outbursts and sobs.

It was almost sunset when we got out of the car. I smelled the healing salt air and felt warmth on my body. Topaz water glistened, and rolled over my restless brain. I let my bare feet sink into soft, powdery sand. I didn't deserve such pleasures.

Our Father was standing by the water's edge, waiting. I knew he would be there.

I felt something brush along the inside of my palm. Ollie's hand was like a whisper. Like a butterfly's wings. His small hand didn't belong in mine. He didn't belong to me, at all. It was time to let go. Ollie did not look back, but walked to the sea.

Ollie walked toward the Father and into pure white foamy waves. A child who could have been mine except for a choice I had the "right" to make.

Ollie might have been a girl. I don't know. I had raised boys, and the familiarity of them caused me to think in terms of another son.

My husband didn't want another mouth to feed. Another burden. Our marriage was on a downhill slide. I was terrified of being left alone with three children. I didn't think I could find a job. I didn't want to leave my children with a stranger. I had so many excuses and so many reasons to make "the choice."

The dark-skinned man reached out his hand to my child. His presence glowed and I could feel his love. His peace surrounded me as he rested his kind dark eyes upon my heart. He took His child into his arms, held him up to the sky, and dipped him into the water. The two of them laughed in their playfulness and joy. They were washed from head to toe, until they became as clear as the ocean beyond.

I sat on the beach with sand blowing in my face. I watched the sunset and stayed through the black, cold night. And when the morning came, it came with grace.

Printed in the United States
24184LVS00002B/334-351

9 781592 990931